BEAVER TOWERS
THE SERIES

*F*ar away, on a magical island, is a castle called
Beaver Towers. It was once the home of happy
beavers – until they were betrayed by magic. Magic
which called up evil creatures from the world of
shadows. The animals of the island send out a call for
help and Philip, an ordinary boy, finds himself drawn into
the struggle to save them from the powers of darkness.

There are four exciting books in the *Beaver Towers*
series. Here they are in reading order:

Beaver Towers
The Witch's Revenge
The Dangerous Journey
The Dark Dream

Nigel Hinton was
born in London. He has written
fifteen novels, including four prize-
winners, and a number of scripts for TV and
the cinema. He enjoys swimming, walking, films,
reading, watching football and listening to music,
especially 50s rock 'n' roll and Bob Dylan

Some other books by Nigel Hinton

THE FINDERS

For older readers

BUDDY
BUDDY'S SONG
BUDDY'S BLUES

COLLISION COURSE
OUT OF THE DARKNESS

NIGEL HINTON

THE WITCH'S REVENGE

THE SECOND BOOK IN THE BEAVER TOWERS SERIES

Illustrated by Anne Sharp

PUFFIN BOOKS

PUFFIN BOOKS

Published by the Penguin Group

Penguin Books Ltd, 80 Strand, London WC2R 0RL, England

Penguin Putnam Inc., 375 Hudson Street, New York, New York 10014, USA
Penguin Books Australia Ltd, 250 Camberwell Road, Camberwell, Victoria 3124, Australia
Penguin Books Canada Ltd, 10 Alcorn Avenue, Toronto, Ontario, Canada M4V 3B2
Penguin Books India (P) Ltd, 11 Community Centre, Panchsheel Park, New Delhi – 110 017, India
Penguin Books (NZ) Ltd, Cnr Rosedale and Airborne Roads, Albany, Auckland, New Zealand
Penguin Books (South Africa) (Pty) Ltd, 24 Sturdee Avenue, Rosebank 2196, South Africa

Penguin Books Ltd, Registered Offices: 80 Strand, London WC2R 0RL, England

www.penguin.com

First published by Abelard-Schuman Limited 1981
Published in Puffin Books 1995

025

Text copyright © Nigel Hinton, 1981
Illustrations copyright © Anne Sharp, 1995
All rights reserved

The moral right of the author and illustrator has been asserted

Set in 11/14 pt Monophoto Ehrhardt by Rowland Phototypesetting Ltd, Bury St Edmunds, Suffolk

Printed in England by Clays Ltd, St Ives plc

British Library Cataloguing in Publication Data
A CIP catalogue record for this book is available from the British Library

ISBN 0–140–37061–7
ISBN-13: 978–0–14–037061–4

www.greenpenguin.co.uk

MIX
Paper from
responsible sources
FSC® C018179

Penguin Books is committed to a sustainable future for our business, our readers and our planet. This book is made from Forest Stewardship Council™ certified paper.

For Haze

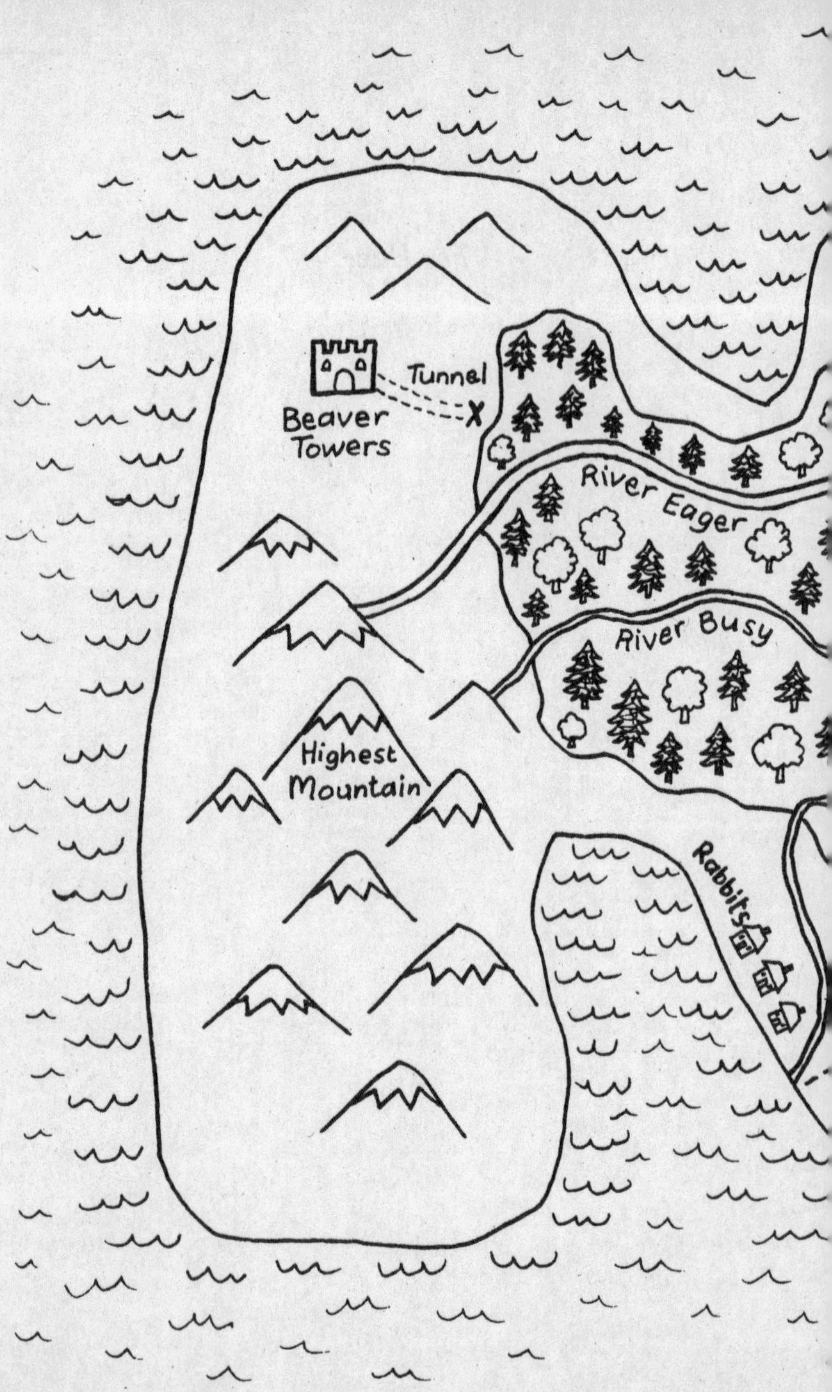
Tunnel
X
Beaver Towers
River Eager
River Busy
Highest Mountain
Rabbits

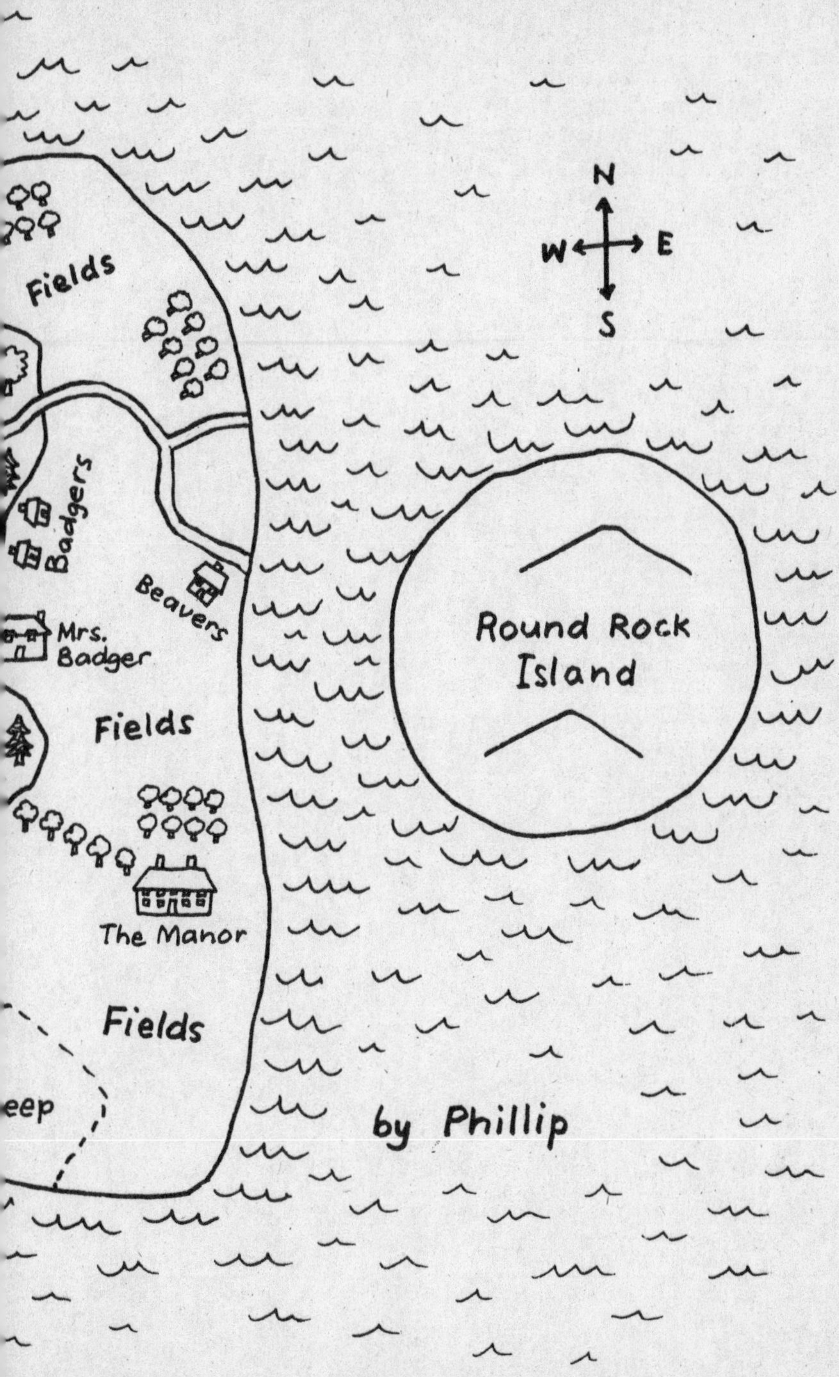

N
W
E
S
Fields
Badgers
Beavers
Mrs. Badger
Fields
The Manor
Fields
eep
Round Rock Island
by Phillip

CHAPTER ONE

On an island in the middle of the sea, a long way from anywhere, a small beaver was rocking up and down on a swing. His name was Baby B.

If you could have looked down on the island at that moment, you would have shouted, 'Look out, Baby B! There's something horrible coming just over the hill. Quick, run away.'

But you weren't there, so Baby B went on swinging happily.

He had been happy all day. His grandad, Mr Edgar Beaver, had taken him to see their old friend Mrs Badger. They had eaten a delicious lunch, then the grown-ups had decided to have a little snooze. So Baby B went into the garden to have a swing.

He loved to swoop up and down as high as he could. And while he was swinging he always made up songs. Today's song went like this:

'Zoom, zoom, buzz, whee
I am flying like a bee.
Zoom, zoom, buzz, why
Am I being like a fly?'

The 'Zoom, zoom, buzz, whee' bits were for when he was going forwards. The other bits were for when he was going backwards.

Sometimes Baby B stopped singing and shouted, 'Look at me, robin, I'm as highest as you!'

The robin was sitting on the branch above the swing. He liked it best when Baby B was singing because he could whistle along to the tune.

Baby B stopped singing and put all his effort into making the swing go higher. He pumped his little legs backwards and forwards and the swing climbed up and up.

'Look at me, robin,' he shouted, 'I'm as highest as . . .'. And then he stopped. His mouth fell open with fright and his eyes nearly popped out of his head.

Something that looked like a huge brown snake was wriggling down the hill behind Mrs Badger's house. It was moving very fast. Nearer and nearer. And it was enormous. Already its head was near the house and its body stretched all the way back to the top of the hill.

Suddenly the head of the snake came round the side of the house and started moving across the grass towards the tree. As it came nearer, Baby B saw that it wasn't a snake at all. Something was pushing the earth up out of the ground.

'Help, it's an earthquaker,' he shouted.

The tree began to tremble and there was a horrible hissing and rumbling. Baby B hung on to the swing and squeezed his eyes shut. A nasty smell like bad eggs and drains floated up to his nose.

The noise faded away and the shaking stopped.

Baby B's heart was beating fast and the horrible smell was making him feel sick. When he opened his eyes, the long line of earth stretched right underneath the swing and away into the forest behind him.

He jumped off the swing and started running to Mrs Badger's house. Suddenly, he felt something wet and squelchy under his feet. He stopped and looked. Thousands of pink, slimy worms were wriggling and squirming their way up out of the earth.

'Help! Wigglers!' shouted Baby B and he jumped and hopped and skipped his way to Mrs Badger's front door.

He burst into the parlour shouting and screaming.

'Wake up. Wake up. It's an earthquaker and wigglers. Look out, they're coming.'

He jumped into Mrs Badger's lap and hid his head under her apron.

CHAPTER TWO

Mrs Badger and Mr Edgar woke up with a start.

'What? Eh? What?' mumbled Mr Edgar.

'Baby B, what are you doing?' said Mrs Badger and she lifted up her apron.

Baby B couldn't speak. He pointed outside and then pulled the apron down over his head again.

'Baby B, stop this silliness,' said Mrs Badger and she lifted him off her lap and stood him on the floor.

He still couldn't speak but he took Mr Edgar's paw and pulled him to the door.

'Well, I'll be blowed,' said Mr Edgar when he saw the long line of earth and the thousands of worms.

'It was an earthquaker, Grandpa,' Baby B said, finding his voice at last. 'I was just doing swinging and I thinked it was a snake and it tried to get me but it missed. Then all of them wigglers came and started wiggling and they were all squelchy when I treaded on them.'

'Oh dear me, an earthquake,' Mrs Badger gasped.

'Now, now, hold your horses, you two,' Mr Edgar said as he stepped out of the door to have a closer look. 'We've never had an earthquake on the island. Besides, they make holes in the ground, but this – this looks as if . . .' he bent down and picked up some of the loose earth . . .'this looks as if something has gone along under the ground and pushed up the earth.'

'Perhaps it was a mole,' said Mrs Badger.

'I don't think so,' said Mr Edgar. 'Moles only make little hills. I can't think of any animal that could do this.'

Mr Edgar scratched his head. 'I wonder how far it stretches? And what's that horrible smell? Whatever it was must have almost choked the worms as well as giving them a dratted fright.'

'It didn't give me a dratted fright,' Baby B said.

'Baby B, how many times have I told you not to use that word? Really, Mr Edgar, you shouldn't encourage him.'

'Sorry, Mrs Badger – just slipped off me tongue. Won't happen again,' Mr Edgar said and then he quickly changed the subject. 'Look at the robin – he's never seen so much food in his life.'

The robin was standing in the middle of all the wriggling worms. He was turning his head from side to side as if he wasn't sure where to start. Finally, he chose the fattest worm he could see. He picked it up in his beak and flew off to eat it in private. In less than a minute he was back for another.

'Hold on, Sergeant Robin,' Mr Edgar said. 'Your eyes are bigger than your tummy. I don't want you getting fat. I've got an important job for you to do.'

The robin looked sadly at all the tempting worms, then flew on to Mr Edgar's shoulder.

'Now listen, Sergeant, I want you to fly off and follow this line of earth. I must know where it comes from and where it goes to. Understand?'

The robin bobbed to show that he knew what to do, then flew off. They watched him until he reached the top of the hill and disappeared behind it.

'Well,' said Mrs Badger, 'while we're waiting, we may as well go inside and have a cup of something.'

Baby B sat on the window seat so that he could watch out for the robin. Mr Edgar said he'd make the tea, so Mrs Badger sat in her rocking-chair. In a couple of minutes Mr Edgar came back with tea for himself and Mrs Badger and a glass of milk for Baby B.

'I took the liberty of cutting three slices of your wonderful chocolate cake,' Mr Edgar said. 'I hope you don't mind, Mrs Badger.'

'Not at all,' she replied. 'I made it specially

when I knew you were coming. Be careful not to drop crumbs, Baby B.'

Baby B sat with his plate on his lap and made sure that not a single crumb was wasted.

'Well, Mr Edgar, what do you make of it all?' asked Mrs Badger when they had finished their drinks and cake.

'Delicious as ever, Mrs Badger, my dear.'

'No, I mean the earth and the worms.'

'Ah, that,' said Mr Edgar. 'Well, I don't want to say too much before I hear what the robin has found out. But if it turns out to be what I think it is, I'm afraid we've got trouble on our paws.'

Mr Edgar's voice was so serious that Baby B ran over to sit on Mrs Badger's lap.

He looked at his paws to see if there was any trouble on them. 'I'm not scared,' he said.

But he was.

CHAPTER THREE

All the worms had gone down into the ground by the time the robin got back. He looked so disappointed at missing such a lovely feast that Mrs Badger gave him a small slice of cake instead. He pecked away at the cake and told them what he had seen.

The line of earth went from one side of the island to the other. It started near the Manor where Baby B lived, then went past Mrs Badger's house all the way to Mr Edgar's castle, Beaver Towers. After that it went straight towards the sea. At the edge of a high cliff, the line stopped. There was just a large hole where something had come out of the ground.

'So,' said Mr Edgar, when the robin had finished, 'she didn't find what she was looking for.'

'She? Who are you talking about?' asked Mrs Badger.

Mr Edgar took a deep breath and said quietly, 'I think we have had a visit from Oyin.'

'Oyin! Oh no!' gasped Mrs Badger and she looked at the window as if the terrible witch might be outside at that very moment.

'Is she c–c–come to hurting us, Grandpa?' Baby B whispered and his big eyes began to fill with tears.

'Fiddlesticks,' Mr Edgar said and lifted the little beaver on to his lap. 'Now don't you worry your head about Oyin. You heard what Sergeant Robin said – if it was her, she's come out of the ground and gone flying off somewhere else.'

'Why did you think it was her?' Baby B said.

'Oh, just putting two and two together. It was that horrible smell mostly. It reminded me of the smell she left behind at Beaver Towers. It's the kind of smell that comes from the World of Shadows. No wonder those poor worms had to come up for air.'

'You're right,' said Mrs Badger. 'I knew I'd smelled it before. It was the night all those growlers jumped on the fire.'

They shivered as they remembered that night. The witch, Oyin, had come to try and capture Beaver Towers so she could live there as Queen. She had caught nearly all the animals and she was going to make her growlers throw them on a big fire. Then, at the last moment, her plan had gone wrong. She had been called back to the World of Shadows and all the growlers had jumped on the fire and died.

'Will the growlers come back?' Baby B asked.

'No fear,' said Mr Edgar. 'They're all burned up for ever – and good riddance to bad rubbish.'

'But Oyin . . .' Mrs Badger whispered.

'Ah, now she's a different kettle of fish. She must still be furious about what happened – witches don't like having their plans ruined. I dare say she'd like to get her evil claws on the person who stopped her from getting control of Beaver Towers.'

'Me?' said Baby B.

'No,' laughed Mr Edgar, 'I don't mean you. If it had been anyone on the island, she wouldn't have gone away. No, she was looking for someone else. Someone who has been to the Manor and Beaver Towers and here, to Mrs Badger's house. Remember, the robin said the line only went near those three buildings.'

'She was searching for Philip,' Mrs Badger said and then looked at Mr Edgar. 'I'm sure of it.'

'I'm sure of it, too,' Mr Edgar said.

'Flipip,' Baby B shouted and jumped up and down happily. 'Hooray for Flipip.'

Even though he couldn't say his name properly, Philip was the best friend Baby B had ever had. The young boy had been brought to the island by mistake when one of Mr Edgar's spells had gone wrong. It was he who had stopped Oyin and saved everyone from the fire and the growlers. When Philip had gone home again, Baby B had been very sad. Every day he wished they could have some more adventures together.

'Flipip's coming,' Baby B shouted, 'and he's going to bonk silly old Oyin on the head. Hooray!'

'Ssh, Baby B. Your grandpa doesn't mean that Philip is coming. He means that Oyin has gone to look for him. That's it, isn't it, Mr Edgar?' said Mrs Badger.

''Fraid so. And if she finds him, he's going to be in great danger because he rescued us.'

Baby B stopped jumping up and down and looked at his grandfather. 'Can't we reschew him?' he said.

'Easier said than done, young 'un,' Mr Edgar replied.

'Grandpa, we've got to. He reschewed us so we've got to reschew him or it's not fair.'

'Baby B is right,' Mrs Badger said. 'Philip did us a favour. We must help him if he's in danger.'

'I know, I know, Mrs Badger, but how?'

'Do it like you done before,' said Baby B. 'Send the cloud.'

'Good idea, young 'un. I'll beetle back to Beaver Towers and get the magic going. Let's just hope we're not too late. Now that Oyin knows he's not here, she'll be looking everywhere. And if she finds him . . .' Mr Edgar stopped and stood up. 'Get my coat, will you, Baby B – there's no time to lose.'

CHAPTER FOUR

The thunderstorm started as soon as Philip left school. He stood under a large tree when the rain got really heavy. Lightning lit up the dark sky and the thunder boomed and rumbled along the wet street.

Suddenly he remembered that lightning sometimes hits trees. He ran out from under the tree and kept running until he got to the baker's shop. He stood in the doorway and drops of water ran down his face from his soaking hair. He watched the cars splashing through the puddles.

Now he was safe, Philip began to enjoy the storm. The wind was blowing the rain in sheets. Flashes of lightning crackled down. The thunder made the whole road jump.

It was one of the best storms he had ever seen. It was almost as wild as the one Oyin had sent so that the growlers could attack Mrs Badger's house. He thought about how the growlers had nearly caught him. He could almost see their evil eyes and snapping yellow teeth. A drop of rain ran down his neck. He shivered.

Oyin, the growlers, Beaver Towers. It all seemed so far away. He would love to see Mr Edgar and Mrs Badger; and how he missed Baby B. He wished he could go back there for a few days. But most of all he wished his mother and father would believe him about Beaver Towers.

When he got back home after his adventures on the island, there had been terrible trouble. He had been missing for three whole days and his parents had been out of their minds with worry. As soon as he started to tell them what had happened, he knew how strange it must sound. Being carried off to an island on a kite. Helping animals to fight horrible monsters called growlers. Meeting a boy who looked like him and then finding out it was really a witch.

No wonder they hadn't believed him.

They had got angry and told him to stop telling lies. Then, when he had kept on telling the same story, they had taken him to see a doctor. But the doctor had said that there was nothing the matter with him and that it was best to forget all about it. Everybody said it had just been a dream but Philip knew it had been real. As real and true as anything.

When the storm stopped, Philip left the doorway and walked home. The clock outside the station said nearly five o'clock. He was late. He began to run. When he turned into his road, his father's car was parked outside the house. There was a boy standing next to the car. Philip wondered if it was one of his friends.

He looked up and down the road carefully. There was no traffic so he crossed. When he looked towards his father's car again the boy had gone.

Philip ran along the pavement to his house. There was no sign of the boy. He opened the garden gate and noticed a faint smell of something horrible. Perhaps the rain had blocked up the drains.

He went round the side of the house and opened the kitchen door. His father and mother were sitting at the table.

'Hello,' Philip said. 'You're home early, Dad.'

'You're late. Where have you been?' his mother asked and she looked angry.

Philip started to tell them about the storm and how he had stood in the baker's doorway.

'We want the truth,' his father said, standing up quickly and walking towards Philip.

'It is the truth. It was a terrible storm and . . .'

'I know about the storm, but what I want to know is why you weren't at school this afternoon.'

'I was, Dad.'

'Don't tell me lies!' his father shouted. 'I saw you in town. I looked out of my office window and you were walking along the pavement. I opened the window and called you, and you ran away. Now, what were you doing?'

'It wasn't me. I was in school. Honest.'

'Philip, I want the truth.'

'It *is* the truth. It *is*. Ask Miss Coppell – she'll tell you. She read us a story and then we did History. It was all about the Romans. Ask Miss Coppell.'

'That's exactly what I will do. And if you're telling us lies like all that other stuff about witches and animals – I warn you . . .'

While his father went out into the hall to phone, Philip stood in the kitchen. His mother sat at the table and didn't say anything. Philip's face was burning.

After a couple of minutes, his father came back carrying the telephone directory. No one had answered at the school. His father looked up Miss Coppell's home number and went out again. There was a long pause, then he heard his father's voice:

'Miss Coppell? Sorry to disturb you at home. This is Philip Tate's father. Philip says that he was at school this afternoon but I saw him in town and I . . . He *was* in school. I see . . . I must have made a mistake . . . Yes. Well, thank you – that's taken a weight off my mind . . . Yes . . . Thank you again. Goodbye.'

'Well, that's extraordinary,' his father said, when he came back. 'I'm sorry, Philip. Miss

Coppell says you were in school all afternoon. I can't understand it – that boy looked just like you. Anyway, my mistake. Sorry about the bad temper.'

His mother kissed Philip and said, 'Well, let's forget all about it. You hop upstairs and change and I'll make your favourite for tea – pancakes.'

Philip was pleased that the mistake had been cleared up. He ran upstairs and started to change.

Fancy his father seeing a boy who looked . . .

Suddenly a cold shiver ran down his back.

. . . a boy who looked exactly like him.

It was just like that terrible time in the library at Beaver Towers. A boy who looked just like him – but it hadn't been a real boy. It had been Oyin. Philip felt weak as he remembered how the boy's face had melted and become the awful face of a witch.

Another shiver ran down his back.

He was scared.

CHAPTER FIVE

Philip pulled his clothes on quickly and ran downstairs before he could become more scared. His mother was making the pancakes and his father was out in the garden talking to Mr Tibbs next door. Philip read a comic.

'Well, a lot of strange things are going on today,' his father said as he came in and sat at the table. 'Mr Tibbs has just shown me a big hole in his garden. It's so deep you can't see the bottom. Looks just as if something has pushed its way up out of the ground.'

'How did it happen?' Philip's mother asked as she served the pancakes.

'No idea. Mr Tibbs says it wasn't there this morning. Must have happened sometime during the day. I've never seen anything like it.'

As soon as Philip had finished his tea, he ran outside and climbed up the fence to look over into Mr Tibbs's garden.

There was the hole – right in the middle of the lawn.

Philip leaned over the fence as far as he could and then noticed the horrible smell. It was the same one he had smelt outside his house, but much stronger here. It made him feel sick and, somehow, it reminded him of something.

He went back inside to talk to his father but he wasn't there.

'He's gone back to the office to do some work he should have done this afternoon,' his mother explained.

'There isn't half a horrible smell outside, Mum.'

'Is there, dear? Well, don't go out then – perhaps there's a drain broken somewhere.'

'No, it's not quite like drains. It's like ... I don't know.'

Philip sat in the front room and tried to read his comic but he kept thinking about the smell. Where had he smelt it before? It was ...

It came to him in a flash and he dropped the comic in fright. It was the smell of Oyin. The whole of Beaver Towers had smelt of it that night she was there.

He ran into the kitchen shouting, 'Mum! Mum!'

'What is it?'

'It's not drains – it's Oyin.'

'It's what?'

'Oyin. You know – the witch. The one I told you about. She came to Beaver Towers and ...'

'Philip. Stop it!'

'But Mum, it's true. And that boy Dad saw wasn't me, it was her.' Philip was shouting and he could feel tears of fear filling his eyes.

His mother grabbed his shoulders and shook him. 'Stop that nonsense at once, Philip. I've told you before not to keep on telling those lies. You're just a naughty boy.'

The telephone rang and his mother let go of him and went to answer it. Philip looked out of the kitchen window.

The hole. The storm. The smell. The boy who looked like him. It had to be Oyin. She was here in the town looking for him. Perhaps the boy he had seen outside his house had really been her. Why was she here? What was she going to do to him?

His mother came back into the room. Philip tried to say something but she raised her hand and said, 'Now, no more – I'm warning you. If I hear another one of your silly lies, I shall get really angry.'

Philip closed his mouth and his mother went on, 'That was Mrs Jessup on the phone. She's not very well and she's asked me to go over there and do a few things for her.'

Philip watched as his mother put on her coat.

'Can I come, Mum?'

'I'd rather you didn't, Philip. You know how ill she is. She doesn't want any noise.'

'Oh, please, Mum. Let me. I don't want to stay

here all by myself. Please Mum – Oyin might come.'

As soon as he said it, he knew it was a mistake.

'That settles it. I warned you. You stay right here, my lad. And not another word out of you.'

She took some food out of the fridge and put it in her basket. Philip followed her to the front door.

'Mum,' he said.

'No!'

She opened the door and stepped outside.

'Perhaps this will teach you not to tell lies,' she said. 'You can stay by yourself for half an hour and think about what I've said.'

She pulled the door closed behind her. Philip heard her footsteps go away down the path. The garden gate clanged and she was gone.

He was alone in the house.

CHAPTER SIX

He wanted to cry. Half an hour. Anything could happen. Oyin could come and now there was no one to stop her. Perhaps she was outside, watching the house.

He bolted the front door and ran through into the kitchen and locked the back door, too. He was just about to sit at the table when something scratched on the back door. He froze and waited.

Scratch, scratch. There it was again. Scratch, scratch. Something was trying to get in from the garden.

The scratching came again, followed by a bark. That wasn't Oyin. It sounded like Megs. He ran to the door and unlocked it. Megs bounded into the room, wagging her tail.

'Megs, oh Megs, you good dog,' he shouted and patted and hugged her. 'Good old Megs, you'll stay with me, won't you?'

Megs barked and ran round the table, then came back and licked his face and wagged her tail. Philip stood up and locked the door again.

'Come on, girl,' he said and Megs followed him into the front room.

He sat on a chair and patted Megs.

'You believe me, don't you, girl? And you won't let old Oyin get me, will you? You'll bark and growl at her until she goes away. Please say you will.'

Megs wagged her tail and looked at him with her lovely brown eyes. Philip was glad she was there, but he knew she wouldn't be much use if Oyin came. His father always said Megs was such a softie that she would run away if a burglar tried to break into the house. She was the most gentle, lovable dog in the world but she wasn't very brave.

Oh, if only Mr Edgar was here with his magic books – he would know what to do.

Philip got up and crept over to the window. He pulled the curtain a bit and looked out. There was Mr Nelson coming home from work. Perhaps he could run out there and ask for help. What an idea! He could just imagine what Mr Nelson would say if he ran out shouting, 'Help, there's a witch trying to get me.' The poor man would probably think he was mad. Mr Nelson went into his house.

There was another man walking down the road. Philip had never seen him before. Perhaps it was

Oyin. She could turn herself into any shape she wanted.

The man walked past the house and went round the corner.

How long had his mother been gone? Ten minutes? She had said she would only be gone for half an hour. Another twenty minutes to go. Perhaps she would come back sooner. Hurry up, Mum, please!

Something wet touched his hand and he jumped with fright. It was only Megs wanting to be patted. He stroked her head and kept looking out of the window.

The street was empty now. Just a few cars parked down the road. Could Oyin turn herself into a car? Philip started to laugh at the silly idea but then he stopped. It wouldn't be very funny to be chased by a car.

Besides, everything that had happened at Beaver Towers would have seemed silly if he didn't know that it was true. His friends said that magic was silly and that witches were silly. Well, they wouldn't think Oyin was silly if they saw her. Not one little bit silly. She was evil and horrible and scaring and she was real.

And his parents said he was being silly when he told them he had been carried across the sea on his dragon kite. But that was true, too.

If only he could do it now. If he could just run upstairs and take the kite and fly back to Beaver Towers and Baby B. But he couldn't. It didn't work without the little round cloud and the only person who could send that was Mr Edgar.

Philip peeped out of the window again. No one there.

RING – RING.

Philip nearly jumped out of his skin as the telephone rang. He stepped back and trod on Megs' paw. The poor dog yelped and ran across the room.

'Sorry, girl. Sorry, Megs,' he said, and he patted her gently as he walked to the phone. Perhaps it was his mother or his father. He would tell them to come home quickly. He went into the hall and picked up the phone.

'Hello,' he said.

There was silence at the other end.

'Hello,' he said again.

Still, no one spoke and he suddenly became afraid. He knew who it was – Oyin.

He could almost feel her evil coming out of the phone. He slammed it down. His knees were shaking. She had rung to make sure he was there. He just knew it.

She was coming.

Somewhere outside, she was already coming towards the house.

CHAPTER SEVEN

Philip picked up the telephone directory. He turned the pages, looking for Mrs Jessup's number. He would ring his mother and tell her he was ill. Tell her anything to make her come home. He had just found the number when Megs began to bark and growl. He dropped the book and ran into the front room.

Megs was at the window, barking at something outside. Philip peeped through the curtains. An old lady was standing on the other side of the road, looking straight at the house. She was dressed in a long, black coat that went all the way to her feet. A big, black hat was pulled down over her eyes and her whole face was in shadow.

She stepped off the pavement and the light shone on her face. Philip gasped. It was Oyin.

Megs whined and ran away from the window to hide behind a chair. Philip dashed out of the front room and up the stairs. At the top of the stairs he stopped and looked down at the front door.

He heard the garden gate creak open. There was a long pause, then the knocker banged on the door. He could see a dim shape through the glass. The knocker banged again. Philip stood still.

Slowly, the letter-box opened. Philip held his breath and pressed himself back against the wall.

Long, bony fingers started to come through the letter-box. They moved around like the legs of a spider. Oyin was trying to reach the lock. The whole hand was there now. Then the wrist. Then a thin arm, twisting and tapping its way towards the lock. In a minute she would find it and open it.

Philip ran into the bedroom and closed the door. There wasn't even a lock on this door. He would have to try and block it with something. He pulled the bed round and pushed it hard up against the door. Then he looked for something else. The chair. His dragon kite was on it. He put the huge kite on the floor then grabbed the chair and put it on top of the bed.

There was a click from downstairs and he heard the front door open. Oyin was in the house.

He tried to hear what she was doing but all he could hear was the thump-thump of his heart. He stared at the door. At any minute the door-knob would turn and she would try to come in.

Suddenly there was a loud tap at the window. Philip spun round expecting to see Oyin but it was the dragon-kite. It had left the floor and was knocking against the window as if it wanted to get out.

Philip dashed to the window and pulled the kite away. What was happening? Perhaps Oyin was in the garden. He looked down. It was nearly dark but he could see that the garden was empty. If it wasn't Oyin's magic, what had made the kite move? He looked up and saw it – the little round cloud. Mr Edgar's magic cloud. There it was, bobbing up and down just above the window.

The kite was pulling hard. It wanted to get out. It wanted to fly off with the cloud. And Philip could go with it. It would take him to Beaver Towers like last time. He would be safe.

Quietly, Philip swung the window open. The kite pulled and tugged and he had to hold it tight. It was so big that he would have to slide it out on its side.

He pushed the window some more and it banged loudly against the outside wall. There was the sound of footsteps running up the stairs. Oyin had heard the noise and was coming.

Philip glanced at the door and he felt the kite slip out of his hands. When he looked, the cloud and the kite had gone. He leaned out of the window and saw them already flying high above the house.

'No!' he shouted. 'Come back. Kite, come back.'

The door knob was beginning to turn. He could see the bed start to shake as Oyin pushed from the other side of the door. The bed began to move as the door slowly opened.

He climbed onto the window-sill. It would be better to jump from the high window than let Oyin get him. He felt a breeze blow his hair and he looked up. The kite and the cloud were diving towards him.

He looked at the door. Oyin's hands were coming round the edge and the bed was sliding. The wind grew stronger. It was almost pulling him out of the window. The kite was coming.

He reached up and grabbed hold of it as it passed. His feet left the window-sill and he closed his eyes. The wind blew and he could hardly breathe.

He heard a horrible scream as Oyin burst into the room, then he felt himself rushing up and up.

When he opened his eyes, he was already too high to see which house was his. The whole town was just a group of twinkling lights below him.

He was safe.

CHAPTER EIGHT

The kite flew higher and faster than the first time it had taken him, but Philip wasn't afraid. The cloud knew the way to go and the kite would carry him safely.

After a while, the long tail of the kite wrapped itself round him. He knew that was the sign for him to rest his arms. He let go of the wooden cross-piece. The tail tightened round him comfortably and he swung gently under the kite. He closed his eyes and let the kite rock him to sleep.

When he heard the whisper of waves he opened his eyes but it was too dark to see. Then the moon broke through a dark band of cloud. Far, far below, the sea danced and shimmered in the silvery light. Philip watched the patterns of light shake and shiver on the water until his eyes grew heavy and tired.

The next time he woke up, it was morning.

The sun was shining in a clear blue sky. He reached up and held on to the kite. The long tail unwrapped itself from round him and fluttered up to hop and skip in the breeze.

In less than an hour Philip caught sight of the islands. There was the large one that looked like the letter 'N', and, by its side, was the small one that looked like an 'O'.

The kite began to glide down towards the large island. The lower it flew, the more Philip could see. There was the forest and there were the mountains. And there, standing on a rock, was Beaver Towers.

'I'm back,' Philip shouted, as the kite glided in a big circle round the castle.

The little round cloud turned and flew off across the forest. The kite followed. Lower and lower they flew until Philip's feet were nearly touching the tops of the trees. And then, below him, he saw Mrs Badger's house at the edge of the forest.

'Wheeeeee!' Philip yelled in excitement, as the kite dived towards the garden. When he was nearly touching the ground, Philip let go. He looked up and saw the kite and the cloud already flying away.

'Flipip!' a funny little voice squeaked from behind him.

Philip turned round and there was Baby B, high on his swing. As he ran towards the tree, Philip could see what Baby B was going to do.

'No, Baby B,' he shouted, 'don't jump!'

But it was too late. The little beaver had let go of the swing and was flying through the air shouting, 'Flipip!'

Philip held out his arms but Baby B was coming too fast. The next moment he was lying on the grass with all the wind knocked out of him.

'Ow,' he said, rubbing his tummy.

'Crumbs,' said Baby B, rubbing his head, 'your tummy isn't half hard, Flipip.'

'So's your head, Baby B.'

Baby B put his paw in front of his mouth and started to giggle. Soon they were both rolling around laughing and hugging each other with happiness.

When they had calmed down a bit, they went into the house. Baby B explained that Mrs Badger and Mr Edgar had gone to wait for Philip at Beaver Towers.

'But I knowed you will come here,' Baby B said.

'How did you all know I was coming?' asked Philip.

'Easy. Grandpa sended the cloud. Because I saw Oyin and she was an earthquaker. And I was on my swing and then all the wigglers came and so we knew. And Grandpa did his magic. And if you see a biggest snake but it's not a snake it's really an earthquaker, then it's Oyin.'

Philip got Baby B to sit down quietly and explain it all slowly.

'I understand,' said Philip at the end. 'Well, Mr Edgar was right. I was in danger and if he hadn't sent the cloud, I dread to think what might have happened.'

'Oh drat me,' Baby B said suddenly. 'I forgot my manners, and Mrs Badger says I always do, but I don't, but I did this time.' He cleared his throat and became very polite and serious. 'I expect you are very hungry and thirsty, would you like a nice cup of something?'

Philip had to laugh – he knew who had taught Baby B to say this. The little beaver looked and sounded just like dear old Mrs Badger.

'Why, Baby B,' said Philip in the same polite way, 'that would be very kind of you.'

'Don't menchew it. Only I mustn't put the kettle on, in case I tread in the fire.'

Philip filled the kettle and put it on the fire. Baby B rushed round the kitchen getting things ready. He made one or two mistakes, like putting the milk and sugar in the teapot, but at last the tea was made and poured. Philip carried the cups into the parlour and Baby B followed with two plates of chocolate cake.

'Be careful not to drop crumbs, Flipip,' Baby B said, handing over one of the plates. 'Oh drat,' he added, as his own plate fell on the floor spilling cake everywhere.

By the time Baby B had picked up all the pieces and tried to press them together again, Philip had finished eating his slice. He took his cup of tea and sat on the window seat. He looked out at the garden and saw the line of earth that Oyin had pushed up.

It was so good to be back here but perhaps it wasn't as safe as he'd hoped. Oyin had already been here looking for him. He had a horrible feeling that it wouldn't be long before she came back again.

CHAPTER NINE

Baby B was asleep in his chair when Philip saw the robin land on the apple tree. Philip ran out of the cottage door and the robin flew on to his shoulder and pressed his warm feathers against his neck.

'Hello robin,' Philip said. 'I'm so glad to see you again. Is Mr Edgar coming?'

The robin bobbed and flew off towards the fields. Philip followed him to the end of the garden and saw Mr Edgar's old open car coming along the path from the forest.

Mr Edgar was sitting in the driver's seat and Mrs Badger was by his side. The car bumped slowly along, clattering and clanking as loudly as ever. Philip could see the three hedgehogs who always pushed the car and he could hear them shouting 'Heave Ho'.

There was a slight slope down towards the house and the car started to roll a bit faster. The hedgehogs stopped pushing and jumped on the back bumper for a ride. Suddenly Mr Edgar saw Philip.

'Young 'un!' the old beaver shouted, standing up on his seat. 'Splendid. You made it back then.'

He was just about to say something else when the car hit a small bump. Mr Edgar did a neat somersault and landed in a heap in the back seat.

Poor Mrs Badger found herself in charge of a car that was rolling straight towards her front door. She grabbed the steering wheel and twisted it.

The car made a sudden swerve away from the house and started heading towards a large tree.

Mrs Badger screamed and put her paws over her eyes.

'The brake, ma'am! Press the brake!' yelled Mr Edgar.

Mrs Badger took one paw away from her face and pressed the horn. The horn was still honking when the old car rolled gently into the tree.

Mr Edgar, who had just stood up on the back seat, did another somersault. This time it was forwards and, to his great surprise, he suddenly found himself in the front seat again. His large driving goggles were wrapped round his legs but he was pleased to find that he was holding the steering wheel.

'There you are, ma'am, safe as houses,' he said. 'Told you there was nothing to worry about.'

'Mr Edgar. Mrs Badger. Are you all right?' Philip asked as he ran up to the car.

'What? Splendid. Never better. Well, I would be if I could get me dratted legs out of these dratted goggles,' Mr Edgar gasped.

He pulled the goggles up until they were wrapped round his tummy.

'That's better,' he said as he jumped out.

He ran round to the other side of the car and opened the door politely. A very shaken Mrs Badger tottered out of the car.

'Topping drive, eh Mrs Badger? Nothing like it, eh?' he said.

Mrs Badger shook her head, 'No, Mr Edgar, I think I can safely say there is nothing like it – thank goodness! Philip, my dear, I'm so glad you're back.'

She gave Philip a little kiss on his cheek and then limped towards the house.

'Oh well,' sighed Mr Edgar, 'some people just don't take to all this new-fangled speed. Anyway, no real damage done, either to the passengers or to the car. Stout old bus, isn't she? Not a scratch on her,' he said, looking at where the car had bumped into the tree. 'Good heavens, though, where are the Mechanics?'

Philip found the three hedgehogs rolled up into balls behind the car. With a little coaxing he got them to unroll.

'Hello Mick. Hello Ann. Hello Nick,' he said as they stood up and dusted their oily overalls.

'Hello,' they said as they ran to look at the car. They patted the bonnet and started to polish the sides. 'Poor Doris,' they said. 'Poor Doris. Are you all right?'

'I see they still love the car,' Philip laughed.

'The Mechanics? Oh, they're as mad as March hares about her. Polish, polish. Rub, rub. They even sleep in her now. Yes, they do. Bring their blankets down and tuck themselves up in the back seat. They say it's so she won't get lonely at night. Anyway,' Mr Edgar said, taking Philip by the arm and leading him towards the house, 'what about you, young 'un? Good journey? Did you have a visit from our old enemy, Oyin?'

'Oh, yes. And she nearly got me. If you hadn't sent the cloud . . .'

'Well, I guessed something was up. Now come inside and tell me all about it.'

CHAPTER TEN

They all went into the parlour and Philip told them the whole story. When he got to the bit where Oyin tried to get into the bedroom, Baby B was so scared that he hid under Mrs Badger's apron.

'Well, you really had a close shave, I must say,' Mr Edgar said when Philip finished.

'Too close,' Philip said. 'Why did she go to my home, Mr Edgar? What does she want?'

'I expecting she was angry,' whispered Baby B, coming out from under the apron.

'Quite right, young beaver,' said Mr Edgar. 'She was angry. And no wonder. Our friend Philip ruined her plans to get Beaver Towers. I don't suppose her master was too happy about that.'

'Who is her master?' Philip asked.

'The Prince of Darkness, young 'un,' Mr Edgar replied in a low voice. 'The Prince of Darkness.

I'm surprised he didn't destroy Oyin as soon as he found out she had failed in her job. My guess is that he only let her go on one condition.'

A dark shadow seemed to pass across the room and everyone shivered.

'What condition?' asked Philip.

'Well, no sense in keeping the truth from you,' Mr Edgar said, patting Philip's hand. 'She's out to destroy you. She's been here and she's been to your home and she won't stop until she's found you.'

There was a long, long silence. Mrs Badger smiled gently at Philip to try and comfort him. Baby B's eyes filled with tears. Mr Edgar gazed at the fire.

'Where can I go?' Philip managed to say at last.

'Go?' said Mr Edgar. 'Who said anything about going? You're staying here, of course. When there's evil about, friends have to stick together. We've beaten Oyin once, and we can do it again.'

'Hooray,' shouted Baby B, sliding down Mrs Badger's legs and running to Philip. 'I can help. I'm good at helping.'

'First things first, Baby B,' Mr Edgar said. 'We've got to get organized. We'll need to have a proper warning if Oyin comes. That's your job, Sergeant Robin. Fly off round the island and tell all the birds to keep a sharp look out for trouble. The minute any of them notices anything strange, they must sound the alarm.'

The robin flew out of the door at once.

'The next thing,' Mr Edgar went on, 'is to get everyone into Beaver Towers. There's plenty of room and we'll all be a lot safer there. Philip, Baby B – attention!'

Philip and Baby B got up and stood straight and still.

'You must go round the island telling everyone the plan. Tell them not to dawdle. They must pack the things they need and be in Beaver Towers before the sun goes down this evening. Not a moment later, understand?'

Philip and Baby B nodded.

'While you're doing that, Mrs Badger and I will go back to Beaver Towers and get things ready. Now, off you go. And take care – for all we know Oyin could be here at any minute.'

CHAPTER ELEVEN

Baby B had got better at running since the last time Philip had seen him. Philip could only keep up because the little beaver's legs sometimes went a bit too fast and tripped over themselves.

Once, Baby B fell down and sat waiting for Philip to catch up. As he got nearer, he could hear Baby B saying, 'Yes. Yes. No. Yes. No.'

'What are you talking about?' Philip asked, glad of a chance to sit down and have a rest.

'I doing my plants,' Baby B replied.

'What does that mean?'

'It's my lesson, of course. Mr Stripe says I got to do my plants every time I go out.'

'Who's Mr Stripe?'

'He's my smelly old teacher. Only he's not really smelly – only when he makes us do millions work.'

'But why do you say "yes" or "no"?'

'Easy. If I can eat them, I say "yes" but if they

are poisonous, I say "no". Look.' Baby B pointed at some plants near Philip's feet. 'Yes. Yes. Yes. No. Yes.'

'But they all look alike,' Philip said.

Baby B giggled. 'You are funny, Flipip. I bet you don't do very good in your tests at school.'

'We don't have tests about plants . . . We only have tests about Geography and things. Come on, we'd better get going.'

'What's Grogafee?' Baby B asked, taking Philip's hand as they walked along.

'Oh, maps and things.'

Baby B didn't even know what a map was, so Philip told him. Baby B was very interested and he said that Philip ought to make a map of the island.

The more Philip thought about the idea, the better it seemed. A map could be very useful if you were planning things. All he had to do was to keep his eyes open and try to remember where everything was. He would start straight away.

They were walking along by the side of a stream and Baby B told him it was called the River Busy. Philip thought it was a bit small to be called a river but it certainly was busy. The water rushed and bubbled and swirled through the forest.

Soon the trees ended and the stream twisted and turned through open fields. Philip could see three houses ahead of them at the edge of the sea.

'Come on, we got to jump,' said Baby B and he took some steps backwards. He put his head down and galloped towards the stream. The little beaver just cleared the water but he hadn't realized how soft it was on the other side. He landed knee-deep in mud and couldn't move his legs.

'Help, I'm all stuck up,' he shouted. He tried to pull his legs out but he lost his balance and fell face down in the mud.

Philip jumped over the stream and pulled him out.

'Pooh, it's all smelly,' Baby B said, trying to wipe the dirt off his face. 'Oh drat, look at my gungarees. If I go in the sea it will be better. Come on.'

Baby B ran off towards the houses and Philip followed. Baby B knocked on the doors and shouted. Soon there were ten rabbits waiting in a circle to hear the news. Baby B flicked some mud off his whiskers and told them about Oyin coming.

'And Mr Edgar says you mustn't dawggle and you got to pack and be in Beaver Towers. And if the sun goes down it's too late. Quick!'

The rabbits didn't need telling twice. They dashed into their houses and Philip could hear them shouting and banging as they got ready.

Baby B ran down to the sea and stood in the shallows, washing his face and his dungarees. Philip looked out over the bay to the other part of the island and saw the waves crashing against the very high cliffs. Behind the cliffs, tall mountains stretched away into the distance. Already the sun was beginning to sink behind the highest mountain. They must hurry and tell all the other animals.

'Come on, Baby B,' he shouted and then saw the big wave tearing towards the shore. Philip didn't even have time to shout a warning. The wall of green water poured over the little beaver. The wave burst with a crash of white foam and swept up the beach.

Philip peered anxiously as the water ran away. There was no sign of Baby B. He ran to the edge of the sea. Suddenly, there was a big splash and Baby B leaped from under the water and dived towards another wave.

'Hooray,' he shouted. 'Look at me, Flipip.'

Philip was just going to call him back when he saw how well Baby B was swimming. Of course! Beavers were expert swimmers.

'I give you a race,' Baby B yelled and started swimming fast.

Philip ran along the yellow sand, watching the young beaver dive and plunge through the waves like a large brown fish. Finally, Philip couldn't run any more. He sat down on the sand to catch his breath. Baby B came out of the sea and shook water all over him.

'I'm bestest at swimming, can't I?' Baby B said.

'You certainly are.'

Philip got a stick and wrote a big message in the sand.

'What is it?' Baby B asked.

'It says – BABY B IS THE BEST SWIMMER IN THE WORLD.'

Baby B giggled and ran up and down looking at the letters. Then he jumped in the air and ran round the letters again.

'Does it really say that, Flipip?'

Philip nodded and took hold of Baby B's paw. 'Come on, we'd better go and tell the others.'

There were some sheep standing in a field next to the beach. Baby B ran across and started to tell them the news but they just went on munching grass. He jumped up and down and shouted, 'Quick, quick, Oyin is coming,' but the sheep wouldn't listen.

'What can we do, Flipip? Grandpa Edgar says you just can't organdize sheep, they only do what they want. And these ones only want to eat grass.'

'Well, we can't force them to come,' Philip said. 'We've warned them and that's all we can do. Come on, we'll go and tell the others.'

It took nearly two hours to go round all the houses. First they went to the Manor and told Baby B's mother and father. Then they went through the orchards and told some beavers who lived near the River Eager. Finally they took the path back towards Beaver Towers. On the way, they stopped to tell some badgers who lived near Mrs Badger's house.

When they left the badgers, the sky was growing dark. A few stars were twinkling above the trees. The forest was full of black shadows. Baby B gripped Philip's hand tightly.

Suddenly there was the sound of running footsteps.

They stopped in fright but then laughed when they saw the badgers hurrying towards them.

'We thinked you was Oyin,' said Baby B.

'Ssh, don't say that name,' whispered one of the badgers. 'She might hear it and think you're calling her.'

They ran along the path and didn't stop until they were on the drawbridge of Beaver Towers. Philip could see all the animals standing in the courtyard. Mrs Badger was fussing round, handing out steaming hot cups of tea and pieces of cake.

'That's everybody except the sheep,' Mr Edgar said when Philip and Baby B got into the courtyard. 'How long will they be?'

'They won't come, Grandpa. Me and Flipip told them but they didn't listen, would they, Flipip?' Baby B said.

Philip shook his head.

'Oh those silly, stubborn sheep,' said Mr Edgar, looking towards the dark forest, 'they never listen to good advice. Let's just hope they change their minds before it's too late. Anyway, it's time to close up for the night.'

He began to turn a large wheel. Chains clanked

and the drawbridge slowly started to rise. There was a loud boom as the bridge closed in the gateway.

'Come on,' called Mr Edgar, 'let's all go inside and get warm. We've got a lot of plans to make before Oyin comes.'

CHAPTER TWELVE

Everyone felt safe at Beaver Towers. There was a lot of singing and laughing as they arranged beds in the Great Hall. By the time the work was done, they were all hungry. They had a fine meal in front of the fire, then Mr Edgar made them all laugh by telling stories and jokes. At last, tired and happy, everyone went to bed.

The next morning some of the older animals set off round the castle to check that all the doors and windows were safe. Others went out into the fields near Beaver Towers to fetch plenty of food for the kitchens.

'We'll need all the food we can find,' said Mrs Badger. 'You never know, we might have to stay inside the castle for a long time if Oyin comes.'

Mr Edgar decided that the young ones had to go on with their lessons as usual, so one of the rooms was turned into a classroom. Philip was disappointed when he was told that he had to join the others for lessons.

'But, Mr Edgar . . .' he started to say.

'No "buts", young 'un,' said Mr Edgar, 'you go to school at home, so you must go to school here.'

So Philip walked up the stairs to the classroom with Baby B.

'Drat,' said Baby B. 'I thinked we wouldn't do dratted school today. It's not fair.'

Philip sat next to Baby B. There were four other pupils – two young rabbits, a small badger and Nick, the youngest hedgehog of the Mechanics.

Mr Stripe, the teacher, was a very old badger who had a deep growly voice.

'Right,' growled Mr Stripe, 'lessons will go on as usual, Oyin or no Oyin. First of all, we welcome a new animal . . . I mean, a new boy. I expect Philip is a hard worker, so we must show him how hard we can work. First lesson is Tracks. Open your books at page fifty-three.'

Philip opened his book and was amazed to see a page full of strange marks and splodges. Was this some kind of animal writing?

'Now, who knows Number One?' asked Mr Stripe. All the animals put up a paw. 'Yes, Baby B?'

'Weasel,' said Baby B.

'Very good. Number Two?'

'Fox,' said one of the small rabbits, and he shivered at the thought.

'Excellent. Number Three?'

'Fieldmouse,' said the badger.

'Very good. Number Four? Philip, you have a go,' said Mr Stripe, pointing to him.

Philip peered at the funny marks. Baby B put his paw over his mouth and tried to whisper something but Philip couldn't hear. Besides, it was no good pretending to know something if he didn't, so he looked at Mr Stripe and told the truth.

'I'm very sorry, Mr Stripe, but I don't know this sort of writing.'

All the animals started to giggle and Nick nearly fell off his chair.

'I beg your pardon?' Mr Stripe said, and his voice was even more growly than before. 'I am afraid I do not like silliness in my lesson. Now, answer the question.'

Philip could feel a blush creeping up his neck to his face. He didn't know what to say and he was very glad when Baby B started to speak.

'Please Sir, Mr Stripe, Flipip isn't being silliness. He doesn't do Tracks and Plants at his school. But he does Grogafee and everything and he's going to do a mack of the island, aren't you, Flipip? You're good at macks, aren't you?'

'Maps,' said Philip. 'He's right, Mr Stripe. I don't even know what Tracks means. Is it like footprints – I mean, pawprints?'

'A bit, I suppose,' said Mr Stripe, 'but much more difficult than that. Anyone can tell a pawprint. Tracks are marks left when an animal brushes past a rock or a tree or a bush.'

'It sounds very hard. I'm not even sure I could tell a pawprint. And I certainly can't tell plants like Baby B can.'

'Oh dear,' said Mr Stripe, scratching his head. 'Can't even tell a pawprint? Not even plants? What a strange school you must go to. Never mind, just pay attention and try to learn as much as you can.'

Philip tried and tried, but all the marks still looked like strange splodges. He was amazed at how clever Baby B and the others were. They could even tell if the animal that had left the track had been moving quickly or slowly.

The next lesson – Smells – was even harder. They all had to close their eyes and say what Mr Stripe was holding up at the front of the class. Philip sniffed as hard as he could but he couldn't smell a thing. Yet Baby B and the others were able to say things like 'an oak leaf that a snail has crawled on' or 'the tail feather of a young thrush' – and get it right every time.

The lesson about Plants was a bit easier. Philip listened and watched very hard and he tried to remember how to tell the difference between the plants. At the end of the lesson there was a test. All of the animals got their answers right. Then it was Philip's turn. Mr Stripe held up two plants and asked Philip to name them.

He looked carefully at the leaves and flowers,

then said, 'That's Cow Parsnip and that's Fool's Parsley.'

Everybody clapped their paws and Philip felt proud – it was the first thing he'd got right all morning. Mr Stripe gave him a gentle pat on the back and said, 'Well done. Now, which is the one you mustn't eat because it is poisonous?'

All the animals looked at Philip. He pointed to the Fool's Parsley.

'Hooray for Flipip,' shouted Baby B. 'Three cheers for Flipip.'

They all gave three cheers, and even Mr Stripe smiled.

That was the end of school for the day. Philip and Baby B rushed off to see Mr Edgar. They found him in the library, talking to the robin.

'Hello, you two whipper-snappers,' said Mr Edgar. 'Sergeant Robin has just been out round the island. No sign of Oyin yet so we're safe for a while. The minute they see her coming, all the birds are going to fly up into the air to warn us. That's right, isn't it, Sergeant?'

The robin bobbed and whistled as if to say, 'Yes.'

Philip and Baby B sat on the floor next to Mr Edgar's chair and told him about the morning's lessons. Mr Edgar laughed gently when Philip told him he found the work very hard.

'I expect you do, young 'un. But I bet my old grey whiskers you can read and write better than any of them – even dear old Mr Stripe. We animals find it very hard.'

'You can read and write though, can't you, Mr Edgar?'

'Indeed, I can. But it took me years to learn. My father taught me how, and I'm starting to teach Baby B. He knows some of the letters, don't you?'

Baby B nodded. 'Hay, Bree, Flea, C, D, Me, Heff and all them others. But I want to learn macks. Flipip is going to do a mack.'

'He means "map",' Philip said, and he began to explain the idea to Mr Edgar.

'What a topping plan,' Mr Edgar said when Philip had finished. 'You must start it at once. It could help us a lot against Oyin.'

'The only trouble is,' said Philip, 'I haven't seen all the island. I saw a lot of it yesterday with Baby B but I really need another look. Do you think ... well, Baby B and I were thinking ... perhaps you could send for the kite and the cloud. If we could just fly round the island quickly, I could remember everything.'

'Oh no, young 'un – you're not going out there.'

'Oh please, Grandpa. I want to go,' said Baby B.

'No,' said Mr Edgar.

'Oh please. We wouldn't be long,' Philip begged. 'And the robin says Oyin hasn't come. Oh please. And you said a map could help us.'

At last Mr Edgar agreed. He picked up his book of magic and said a few words of the spell.

They went down into the courtyard. In a couple of minutes, there was a rushing of wind and the dragon kite and the cloud flew down from the sky. Mr Edgar lifted Baby B up and put him on Philip's shoulder. Philip took hold of the kite.

'Now, take care,' said Mr Edgar. 'Hold on tight, Baby B. And remember, I want you both back here in half an hour. No longer – promise?'

'We promise,' they shouted as the kite started to rise.

'Goodbye,' they called as it carried them out of the courtyard and away.

Mr Edgar went upstairs to the library. He sat in a chair and tried to read but he couldn't. He got up and paced up and down in front of the fire. Finally, he opened the window and looked out towards the forest. Something in his bones was making him feel uneasy. He wished he could see the kite but there was no sign of it.

He stared and stared. He was still staring when there came the rushing sound of wings.

From every tree and bush in the forest, birds were flying into the sky.

It was the alarm signal.

Oyin was coming.

CHAPTER THIRTEEN

'Wheeeee!' shouted Baby B right into Philip's ear. 'We're as highest as anything, isn't it?'

'Don't jump about so much or you'll fall off,' Philip managed to say, though the little beaver had his paw half over Philip's mouth.

They were over the mountains. Beaver Towers was a long way behind them and it looked like a toy castle. Philip could see the coast on the west side of the island. There were tall, rocky cliffs that plunged straight into the blue sea.

The dragon kite rose even higher and carried them over the top of the tallest mountain. On the other side, it turned left and headed towards the eastern part of the island. They glided over the sparkling water of the bay. There, at the edge of the sea, were the houses where the rabbits lived. Next to them, the little River Busy flowed into the sea.

Philip looked at it all carefully. He must remember as much as he could for the map. The kite swept low over the yellow beach.

'Look, Flipip, it's your writing,' shouted Baby B. 'What is it saying?'

'Baby B is the best swimmer in the world,' Philip shouted back, as they zoomed past the words in the sand.

'It should be saying, "Baby B is the best flier in the world",' Baby B yelled, and then added, 'I can't fall in, can I?'

'Not if you hold tight,' Philip said, and he smiled as he felt the little beaver hug him closer round the neck.

The little cloud suddenly turned inland and danced higher into the sky. The kite wiggled its long tail and followed. Soon they were flying over the tall chimneys of the Manor.

'That's where I live,' said Baby B.

'I know,' Philip replied. 'And look at the orchards – all the trees are in straight lines. You can see everything much better up here, can't you?'

Baby B was going to say, 'Yes', but instead he said, 'Whoops!' and then 'Whee!' as the kite lifted its nose and soared higher.

They were both still laughing at the funny feeling it gave them in their tummies when Philip saw the sheep. They looked like six balls of cotton wool and they were running across the fields towards the forest.

'That's strange,' thought Philip, 'they look as if they are scared, I wonder why?'

The next minute, he knew.

First, there was a loud screaming noise. He turned and looked. Thousands of seagulls were flying up from the small round island just off the coast. They flapped into the air and flew off towards the north. Then came a burst of wings and birdsong from below. Every bird on the island was climbing into the sky.

It was like a rainbow of feathers as birds of different colours flashed past them, chirping and twittering. Philip looked up. The birds were flying around high above the kite. And all the time the air was filled with their cries of alarm.

Suddenly, the noise stopped. The birds dived towards the ground and disappeared into the trees. Philip looked down. Nothing was moving. Even the waves on the sea were still, as if they had been frozen. A cold wind whistled round the kite.

'Is it Oyin?' whispered a frightened voice next to Philip's ear.

'It's just the alarm signal, Baby B. Don't worry. We'll tell the kite to take us home.'

But no matter how loudly Philip shouted, 'Take us back to Beaver Towers,' the kite did not change direction. It flew on as if there was nothing wrong.

'Please, cloud. Please, kite. Take us home!' shouted Philip.

Nothing happened.

CHAPTER FOURTEEN

Philip looked round. There was still no sign of danger. Perhaps the kite and the cloud thought there was still time to show him the rest of the island. He hoped they were right.

Below them was the River Eager. It was bigger than the River Busy and it even split into two parts to flow into the sea. He would remember that for the map.

They passed over some more fields and orchards. Then, at last, the kite turned west again. They were heading back to the castle.

'Another five minutes and we'll be home, Baby B,' Philip shouted. 'Look, we're going to fly along the River Eager, across the forest, and then back to good old Beaver Towers.'

There was no reply.

'What's the matter, Baby B?'

No reply.

Philip twisted his head. The little beaver was

staring out towards the sea. His eyes were wide open with fear. A moment later, Philip saw what Baby B was looking at.

High above the sea, an enormous black bird was hovering in the sky. It was looking down at them. Yellow and green fire shone in the cruel eyes. Needles of light flashed from its long, sharp claws.

For nearly a minute the giant bird seemed to hang there. Then it tucked its wings behind its body and fell towards them like a huge rock. Faster and faster it came. Nearer and nearer. Bigger and bigger. And as it fell, it started to blur.

The black wings changed into a flapping cloak. The claws turned to long, bony fingers. The beak became a pointed nose.

It was Oyin.

Her horrible mouth opened and the sky was filled with a terrible scream. Philip saw her sharp finger-nails stretch towards his face. He closed his eyes.

There was a jerk and he felt the kite rush upwards.

He opened his eyes, but he couldn't see. For a moment he wondered if Oyin's nails had ripped into him. Then he realized that his eyes were being pressed by warm, furry paws.

'I can't see, Baby B,' he shouted.

'Sorry,' said Baby B, as he lifted his paws. 'I thinked we was falling.'

Philip felt the paws grab his ears instead.

'Not my ears, Baby B. Round my neck.'

'Sorry.'

Philip looked down. Oyin was rushing up again. Nearer and nearer.

At the last moment, the kite tipped forward and dived. Oyin made a grab for them but they shot past her too quickly.

'Help!' squeaked Baby B, as the kite tumbled. 'OOOOH,' moaned Baby B as the kite twisted and climbed back into the sky. 'Help Flipip. It's millions wobbly up here.'

'All right, try to climb down. Quick, before Oyin comes.'

Philip held on to the kite with one hand and reached up for Baby B. The little beaver wriggled and slid his way down into the safety of Philip's arms.

'Hold tight, here comes Oyin again,' yelled Philip.

Dodging and climbing. Twisting and diving. The cloud and the kite sped through the air. Each time Oyin attacked, Philip was sure she would catch them. But each time, the kite did a little whirl, or skip, or spin, and danced them away from the witch's hands.

Each time she missed, Baby B hugged Philip tighter and shouted, 'Hooray.'

Philip was just beginning to enjoy the wild helter-skelter rides, when the kite shook. He looked up and saw the long dragon tail flying away by itself. Oyin had pulled it off as she had flown past.

The kite wobbled like a see-saw. Oyin was diving again. The little round cloud started to rise. The kite twitched and tried to follow, but it couldn't. It couldn't fly properly without its tail. It started to fall. Faster and faster it went, spinning towards the ground.

Philip could see the forest coming closer and closer. Branches and leaves whizzed past. The kite tipped as it knocked into a tree. There was a loud ripping sound and they jerked to a stop. The kite was caught on a branch.

The ground was still a long way below but they couldn't just hang there waiting for Oyin to come.

'Hold on tight, Baby B – we've got to jump.' Philip gripped Baby B, aimed himself at a clump of ferns below, then let go of the kite.

He closed his eyes and hoped.

CHAPTER FIFTEEN

Philip expected a bump as they hit the ground. Instead, there was a rustle as they fell through the ferns, then a splash. Cold water closed over them. Philip let go of Baby B and swam upwards. He broke through the surface of the water and gasped for air. Baby B popped up beside him.

They had fallen into the River Eager. It was deep but narrow. The ferns grew so close on each bank that they formed a long green tunnel over the river. They swam to the side and hung on to a tree root that stuck out from the bank.

Baby B was just about to say something when there was a hideous scream. Through the ferns they could just see Oyin. She was sitting on the branch next to the kite.

She looked around to see where they had gone. Then she looked down. They held their breath. She seemed to be staring straight at them. Then she looked away. They must be well hidden beneath the ferns.

Oyin jumped from the branch and flew down to the ground. They could hear her crashing through the bushes searching for them. The bank shook as she passed. Then there was silence.

'We must get away before she comes back,' whispered Philip. 'I think it's best to stay in the water but we must be careful not to make noisy splashes.'

'If we go under the water, it's the bestest.'

'I can't swim very far like that.'

'Hold my leg,' Baby B whispered.

Philip got hold of Baby B's leg, took a deep breath, and dived.

The little beaver's flat tail beat fast and they began to move.

Philip helped as much as possible by swimming with his free arm but Baby B did most of the work. They glided through the water until Philip couldn't hold his breath any longer. He tapped Baby B on the shoulder and they swam to the surface.

They burst into the air. Philip took a breath and down they went again.

When they came up the next time, the river bank was not so high and the ferns no longer hid them.

'Coo, it's too hard enough work. I can't swimming any more,' puffed Baby B.

'I think that's far enough,' said Philip. 'Let's get out.'

They climbed out of the river quietly and looked around. Baby B twitched his nose.

'Can you still smell Oyin?' Philip asked.

Baby B nodded.

'Then we'd better find somewhere to hide until she goes away.'

'I know a place – come on.' Baby B grabbed Philip's hand and they ran quickly but quietly through the trees. Then Baby B ducked down and crawled into some ferns. Philip followed him.

Under the cover of the ferns was an old hollow log. They crawled inside and lay huddled up together.

'It's millions good, isn't it?' whispered Baby B. 'Me and Nick finded it when we did a hiderseek.'

'It's perfect,' said Philip. 'Oyin'll never find us here. We'll wait until it's dark and then get back to Beaver Towers.'

The time passed slowly. Baby B curled up and went to sleep.

Twice Philip heard a terrible shrieking sound coming from a long way away. Oyin must still be looking for them. Philip hoped she would soon give up and go away – but he had a nasty feeling that she wouldn't.

Bit by bit, it grew darker.

In a few minutes he would wake Baby B and they would start the journey through the forest. First, he would check that it was safe.

He crawled out of the log and peered through the ferns.

That was strange. It wasn't as dark as he had thought. In fact, it seemed to be getting lighter.

He stood up and saw a yellow-red glow in the sky. What was happening? Could the sun still be shining? Perhaps it was the light from Beaver Towers.

Then, against the glow in the sky, he saw the black shape of Oyin.

He ducked back into the ferns and watched. She flew low across the forest and dived behind some trees. A moment later she flew up again. Suddenly the trees burst into flames.

She was setting fire to the forest.

There was a coughing sound from inside the log. Baby B came crawling out.

'Help, Flipip, it's all smoky in there.'

'Ssh! It's Oyin. She's starting fires everywhere.'

'Where is she?'

'Over there. Look,' Philip whispered, pointing to where Oyin was diving behind some trees near the river. When she flew back into the air, flames leaped round the trees. Smoke curled up into the night and sparks flew from bush to bush, starting more fires.

There was a horrible cackling laugh. They looked up and saw Oyin flying above the trees. Her evil face was lit by the flames.

'Burn! Burn!' she screamed in delight. She

clapped her hands and, at once, a wind began to blow. The flames grew longer and stretched from tree to tree.

In every direction Philip looked, the forest was on fire.

CHAPTER SIXTEEN

A burning tree crashed to the ground near them. Hot sparks jumped into the air and fell down through the ferns.

'Help! I'm being all toasted,' yelled Baby B as he shook the sparks off his fur. 'Come on, Flipip, let's run.'

'No,' Philip said, pulling Baby B back. 'The fire's all round us – there's nowhere to run. Look – she's up there just waiting to spot us.'

It was true. Oyin was flying backwards and forwards just above the tallest flames. She was laughing and screaming at the terrible fire she had made. And all the time she was watching the ground for any sign of Philip and Baby B.

Another tree creaked and slowly fell down in a mass of flames. Then, above the crackling and roaring of the fire, came another noise. It was the sound of terrified sheep.

'Baaaaaaaa! Baaaaaaaa!'

Suddenly, Philip saw them. The poor things were running through the fire in a terrible panic. Their wool was singed and they were dashing around madly, trying to find a way to safety. They tried one way, then another. Each time, they were beaten back by the smoke and the flames.

'Sheep! Sheep! Over here,' shouted Philip and Baby B but the sheep didn't hear. They charged off in another direction and were hidden by the smoke.

Philip and Baby B waited a few minutes, then Philip decided they'd better get back into the log. They crawled in and sat side by side.

'Flipip,' Baby B said in a quiet, scared voice, 'is all them sheep in the fire?'

Baby B looked so worried that Philip took hold of his paw and said cheerfully, 'No, I bet they found a way out. You know those sheep – they probably charged right out of the forest. I bet they're miles away by now, nibbling grass – don't you?'

Baby B nodded and tried to smile but suddenly big tears started to roll down his furry face.

'I want my mummy,' he sobbed.

'Ssh, Baby B. Don't worry, we'll be all right,' Philip said, squeezing his little paw tighter for comfort.

He tried to make his voice sound brave but he was really very scared. What could they do?

Oyin wouldn't be able to see them now because

of all the smoke but if they left the log they might get burned by the fire. But how long would it be before the log started to burn?

Baby B must have seen how scared Philip was.

'We never going to get out,' he cried. 'And we be all burned up like toast. Oh help.'

Tears fell off his fur like rain and he started to rock to and fro in misery. In fact, he rocked so hard that the whole log started to move.

Philip was just going to tell him to stop, when he had an idea. He started moving in time with Baby B. The log rolled back and forth, faster and faster, and then finally turned right over.

'Look out, it's Oyin,' screamed Baby B in shock.

'No, it's not,' Philip said, and he hugged Baby B to stop him being scared. 'It was us. We did it. This log is round. It rolled over just like a wheel. If we rock hard enough we can make it turn. And once it's turning, we can keep it going by rolling around inside. We'll just roll right through the fire and the flames won't be able to get us.'

'Where are we going?' asked Baby B as he wiped away his tears.

'To the river, of course,' said Philip, and he patted him on the head. 'We're going to be safe.'

'Hooray,' shouted Baby B.

'Right,' said Philip, 'there's not a moment to lose. One, two, three – GO!'

They rocked together. Up and down. Up and down.

The log began to tip.

To and fro. To and fro.

'Harder,' shouted Philip.

The log rocked faster and faster, higher and higher. Suddenly, it rolled. Philip felt himself turn right over.

'Now, keep going,' he yelled to Baby B, and the two of them rolled over and over. And the more they rolled, the faster the log rolled.

It was working. They were rolling across the ground like a huge pencil.

'Whoo!' they both shouted as they tipped over. They bumped and crashed into each other but they didn't mind. All that mattered was to keep the log moving.

Outside, the burning trees went whizzing past all topsy-turvy. One second they could see the bottom of the trees, the next second there was a flash as they saw the tops. Then, back to the bottom again.

Once, there was a bang and a jerk as they knocked against a tree. The log twisted round but kept going. Philip just had time to hope that they were still going the right way, when he felt the log fall.

There was a terrific splash and a rush of water ran into the log. They had done it. They were in the river.

Philip grabbed Baby B and pulled him out of the log. They caught a quick glimpse of the fire, then they dived. Philip got hold of Baby B's leg and they swam with all their might.

They came up for air and saw that they had already left the fire behind. They dived again, just in case Oyin was watching the river, and swam some more.

Soon, Philip found that the water was shallow enough for him to stand up. He put Baby B on his shoulders and walked slowly up the river in the darkness.

At last, they rounded a bend and saw Beaver Towers standing high on the rock.

They climbed out of the water and ran along the path at the edge of the forest. When they were near the main gate, they looked up in the sky. There was no sign of Oyin.

Philip took hold of Baby B's paw and they raced up to the drawbridge. 'Open up,' he called.

'Who is it?' someone said.

'It's us,' they both shouted.

'Who's us?' came the voice again.

'Me,' Baby B yelled, jumping up and down. 'Quick, quick. Oyin will hear us.'

'Is that you, Baby B?' asked the voice.

'Yes, yes. It's me. And it's Flipip. Quick, open the bridge.'

They both looked anxiously at the sky. After all the shouting, Oyin might come at any minute.

There was a grinding noise. Then a creak. The bridge started to come down.

At the same moment they heard something crashing through the forest behind them. They turned and stared in fright. The bushes near them shook and then out into the moonlight charged six black shapes.

'Help, it's growlers!' squealed Baby B and he jumped into Philip's arms.

'Baaa! Baaaa!' said the six black shapes.

It was the sheep.

They were dirty, they were scared, they had lost most of their wool – but they were safe.

'Well,' laughed Philip gently as he patted them, 'you finally decided to come to Beaver Towers after all.'

Baby B cheered and the sheep went, 'Baa!' Then they all ran across the bridge.

In the safety of the courtyard, friendly faces waited for them.

CHAPTER SEVENTEEN

Philip was too tired even to stand up. He sat down next to Baby B in the courtyard while all the animals crowded round asking questions. Baby B was already asleep. Philip tried to talk but he couldn't.

In the middle of all the noise he heard Mr Edgar shouting, 'Hold your horses, let's have a bit of hush. Now, some of you rabbits scuttle off and get some grass for these poor sheep – they look starved. Meanwhile we'll get these other two inside.'

Baby B's mother picked up her sleeping son and carried him into the castle. Mrs Badger and Mr Edgar helped Philip to his feet and walked him slowly to the door.

'He must go to sleep straight away,' said Mrs Badger. 'Put him in the bedroom next to the library, Mr Edgar. I'll heat up some broth. Oh dear me, Mr Edgar, fancy letting them go off like that. I'm surprised at you.'

Mrs Badger went into the kitchen, still grumbling. Mr Edgar led Philip upstairs to a room where two beds had been made up. Baby B was already tucked up in one of them. His mother was stroking his head.

'Poor little chap,' she whispered. 'He'll sleep like a top all night. Really, Mr Edgar, I'm surprised at you – letting these two go off like that. They could have been killed.'

'Yes, I know,' sighed Mr Edgar. 'Now don't you start. I've already had Mrs Badger on at me.'

Baby B's mother patted her son once more and tiptoed out of the room. Mr Edgar turned the oil lamp down until there was just a soft, warm glow. Philip got undressed quickly and slipped into his bed. The sheets were cool and crisp. It was so good to lie down.

'Well,' said Mr Edgar quietly, 'you see what a pickle you've got me into?'

'I'm sorry, Mr Edgar,' Philip said.

'Oh, never mind. No harm done, eh. Now tell me all about it – I'm itching to know.'

Philip lay back on the pillow and told Mr Edgar everything. Mrs Badger came in and gave him some delicious broth.

'Really, Mr Edgar, you must let this boy get some sleep,' she said.

'Nearly finished, Mrs Badger. And stop fussing. He's young and as tough as they come, aren't you lad?'

'Yes, I'm all right, honestly, Mrs Badger,' said

Philip. 'And please don't blame Mr Edgar. It was my fault we went. Mr Edgar said no, but I kept on until he said yes. I wanted to go and so did Baby B. And it was scaring, but it was ever so exciting too.'

Mrs Badger tutted and shook her head but Mr Edgar slapped the side of the bed.

'That's the spirit,' he said. 'Of course it was exciting. Splendid stuff. If I wasn't such an old duffer, I would have gone with you. Nothing like a bit of adventure to get the blood racing. You know that, Mrs Badger. Remember the time when we went climbing in the mountains? You were the maddest madcap on four legs – racing up the steepest slopes. I could barely keep up with you.'

'Really, Mr Edgar,' Mrs Badger said. She tried to sound angry but there was a laugh in her voice and a twinkle in her eye. 'I was young and foolish in those days.'

'That you were, Mrs Badger. And wasn't it fun?'

Mrs Badger gave a growly laugh and put a paw over her mouth. 'It was,' she said. 'Such fun.'

'And who was it who climbed the highest mountain on the island all by herself?' Mr Edgar went on.

'Me,' said Mrs Badger smiling. 'And I'll never forget the telling-off my dear old father gave me when I got back.'

'There you are,' Mr Edgar said, getting up. 'And if you were a few years younger, I bet you'd have wanted to go off with Philip and Baby B, too.'

'Perhaps,' she sighed. 'Perhaps.'

Mr Edgar and Mrs Badger laughed quietly together. Their eyes became dreamy and Philip knew that they were both thinking about the days when they were young.

'Anyway, enough of that,' Mrs Badger said suddenly. 'Look at this poor lad, he's tired out. You must let him rest, Mr Edgar.'

'All right,' Mr Edgar said. 'Well done, young 'un. We're proud of you – and my dozy little grandson, there. Aren't we, Mrs Badger?'

'Yes, yes. Now do come along.'

Mr Edgar patted Philip's head and winked.

'Sleep tight,' he said. 'I'm off to the library to see if I can find a magic spell to stop the fire. Goodnight.'

'Goodnight,' Philip said.

Mrs Badger gave him a little kiss and turned the lamp down even lower. She made sure that Baby B's blankets were tucked round him, then she and Mr Edgar tiptoed out of the room.

The door closed and Philip settled down in the bed. What adventures they'd had today. How soft the bed was. How safe and warm it was in Beaver Towers. He could hear the hum of voices from below. The animals were probably getting ready for bed and talking about what had happened.

Philip stretched and closed his eyes. The next minute, he was fast asleep.

CHAPTER EIGHTEEN

When Philip awoke, it was pouring with rain. He got up and looked out of the window. Some smoke was still drifting up from the forest but there were no flames. The fire was out. Mr Edgar must have made some magic to bring the rain.

Philip started to get dressed and Baby B woke up.

'Hello, Flipip. Oh, I'm starving,' he said, jumping out of bed and giving himself a shake.

Philip was hungry, too. He helped Baby B put on his dungarees, then they started downstairs. There was a large notice hanging from the handle of the library door. It said, 'DO NOT DISTURB. MAGIC SPELLS ARE BEING DONE'.

Baby B climbed on to the banister and slid down to the bottom of the stairs. They rushed into the dining hall and started eating breakfast.

Baby B drank four big mugs of milk and ate

seven slices of bread and jam. As soon as all the animals had finished eating, they came over to Philip and Baby B and asked questions. What was Oyin like? How had they escaped on the kite? How did they get out of the fire?

Philip told the whole story and the animals would have liked to hear it all again but they had to get on with their jobs. Food had to be prepared. The castle had to be swept and cleaned. Mr Stripe reminded the young ones that school would begin as usual in five minutes.

'Me and Flipip don't have to come, do we?' said Baby B a bit cheekily.

'You most certainly do. And don't you go getting too big for your boots,' Mr Stripe said sternly, looking at Philip as well as Baby B. 'Now, go outside and tell Nick to come in. I expect the young rascal is already cleaning that beloved car, Doris.'

Mr Stripe started up the stairs to the classroom and Philip and Baby B went into the courtyard. Sure enough, the Mechanics were there, looking after Doris. Mick was holding an umbrella over her bonnet to keep the rain off while Ann and Nick were polishing as hard as they could.

'Come on, Nick,' called Baby B. 'We got to do smelly school.'

Usually Nick never wanted to leave Doris, but today he rushed up to Baby B and started to talk about Oyin and the kite and the fire. Philip walked up the stairs behind them. He could hear

Baby B boasting again and Nick was believing every word.

'Did you, Baby B? Really, Baby B? You are brave. I wish I could go with you on the kite,' the little hedgehog kept saying as he listened.

Mr Stripe said Philip could spend the time drawing a map of the island and he gave him some paper and some coloured pencils. Nick sat next to Baby B and Philip could hear them whispering all the way through the lessons on plants.

Philip worked hard on the map. He tried to remember where everything was. He drew slowly and carefully. Sometimes he got something wrong and had to rub it out. Bit by bit, it looked more and more like a real map. All the important things were there: the mountains, the rivers, the houses, the forest. He even drew the field where he had first seen the sheep. The poor sheep – what a fright they'd had.

The map took all morning to do. When school finished, Philip wanted to show the map to Mr Edgar but the 'DO NOT DISTURB' sign was still on the library door.

He sat next to Baby B and Nick at lunch. The two of them were still talking about Oyin. Baby B seemed to have forgotten how dangerous and scaring it had all been. He just talked as if it had been good fun.

'Where do you think Oyin is now?' asked Nick.

Philip said he didn't know but Baby B said, 'I

think she lives on Round Rock Island. I bet she does. I bet me and Flipip can go there on the boat. And then we can catch her and everything.'

'Oh, can I come, too?' Nick said to Philip.

'He can, can't he?' Baby B said, bouncing up and down. He bounced so hard that he knocked his plate. Some peas and two pieces of carrot flew through the air and hit Mr Stripe who was sitting at the next table.

'Baby B, stop being a nuisance,' growled Mr Stripe.

Philip made Baby B and Nick finish their lunch quickly. Then he led them outside before they got into more trouble.

It was still raining but Mick and Ann were still in the courtyard polishing Doris.

'I know – let's go on the wall to look for Oyin,' said Baby B.

'Don't you want to polish Doris, Nick?' Philip asked.

'No. Polishing's boring. I want to go with Baby B,' said the little hedgehog.

'Well, all right,' Philip said. 'But be careful on the wall. No leaning over the edge.'

Baby B and Nick ran across the courtyard and up the steps. Philip watched them as they looked over the wall. He could see them pointing and talking.

They seemed happy and they weren't doing anything silly, so Philip decided to go inside, out of the rain. He meant to keep an eye on Baby B and Nick but when he saw Mr Edgar come downstairs, he forgot all about them.

It was only later that he realized what a big mistake he'd made.

CHAPTER NINETEEN

Everybody had eaten their lunch so the dining hall was empty. Philip sat down at a table with Mr Edgar.

'Shall I ask Mrs Badger if there's any lunch left for you?' Philip asked.

'No thank you, young 'un. I couldn't eat a thing. Drat me, but I'm tired. I get more like a useless old duffer every day. There was a time when I could do twenty magic spells a day. But nowadays I'm tired out after just one. Mind you, weather spells are a bit trickier than most.'

'Did you send the rain then?'

'Yes, I did,' said the old beaver looking towards the window. 'Good idea, what? It's put the fire out, all right. Trouble is, it was only meant to rain for an hour.'

'You mean you can't stop it?' asked Philip.

Mr Edgar shook his old grey head. 'I'm 'fraid not. That's why I've been up in the library so long. I thought I must have made the spell too strong. It happens sometimes with magic. That's why you have to be so careful. Anyway, I looked in all the books but I just couldn't find out what had gone wrong. Then it came to me in a flash.'

'What?' said Philip.

'Earth, Air, Fire, Water,' said Mr Edgar. Then he looked at Philip and added in a whisper, 'My spell has been taken over by Oyin. I can't stop the rain because she's put a stronger spell on it.'

Philip glanced at the window. Was it his imagination, or was it darker outside and was the rain getting heavier? He suddenly felt afraid.

'Why would Oyin want to make it go on raining, Mr Edgar?' he asked.

'I told you – Earth, Air, Fire and Water. The four elements.'

'What are they?'

'The oldest magic there is. Everything in the world is made from them. Plants, for example – they grow out of the earth, and they need the fire of the sun, water from the sky and good clean air. Even new-fangled things like that useless car, Doris. The metal she's made of comes from the earth and has to be melted down by fire.

'My guess is that the Prince of Darkness has given Oyin four chances to destroy you. Her first attack was by the tunnel she made in the Earth. The second was in the Air when you were on the kite. The third was by Fire in the forest. Her last chance is Water.'

A blast of wind blew the rain hard against the window.

'Well,' said Philip, 'she didn't get me with the other ways. What happens if she doesn't get me with Water?'

'Then the spell will be broken. She has been given four chances. If she doesn't destroy you, the Prince of Darkness will destroy her.' Mr Edgar smiled. 'Cheer up, young 'un. Just one more attack. If you can survive that, we can say "goodbye" to that old horror, Oyin, for ever.'

'"If" is a very big word, Mr Edgar. Oyin will be very anxious to make sure I *don't* survive. But what's she going to do? Even if she makes it rain for weeks, I don't see how it can hurt me.'

'Good point,' said Mr Edgar. 'Mind you, she certainly seems to be brewing up a big storm. Listen to that wind. It's enough to blow your fur off.'

They were both listening to the howl of the wind and the splash of the rain when they heard something else.

From the courtyard came the sound of a scream.

CHAPTER TWENTY

They rushed outside and saw Baby B's mother running down the steps from the castle wall. She dashed across the courtyard, her fur soaked with rain.

'Baby B,' she gasped, 'he's gone.'

Before she could say anything else, the two hedgehogs, Ann and Mick, ran up shouting, 'Nick! Has anyone seen Nick?'

'They were on the wall,' Philip said.

'They're not there now – I've just looked. I've been everywhere. Oh, Mr Edgar, what are we going to do?' asked Baby B's mother.

'Now, don't panic – they can't have gone far. Let's look inside.'

Philip was the one who saw the wet pawprints. They started by the main door, went across the tiled floor and up the main stairs.

'That's them,' Mr Edgar said. 'Those young rascals never bother to wipe their paws. Now everybody can stop fussing. The scamps are somewhere in the castle. Philip and I will follow the prints and find them.'

Philip raced across the stairs ahead of Mr Edgar. The tracks ran along the corridor and into the library. He opened the door. The pawprints led across the library floor to the bookcases. But Baby B and Nick weren't in the room.

Philip was just thinking that they must have gone into another room when he remembered the secret passage. He had used the passage to get into Beaver Towers when the growlers were living there.

He ran to the bookcase and pulled. Slowly the bookcase opened like a door. Behind it were the steep stone stairs that led down to the tunnel. On each of the steps were wet pawprints.

'Found them?' asked Mr Edgar as he came through the library door.

'Oh, Mr Edgar, they've gone down the secret passage. Look, you can see their pawprints.'

'Drat me, what on earth are those two madcaps up to?' said Mr Edgar. 'Don't they realize the danger?'

'That's just it,' Philip said. 'Baby B and Nick were talking all morning. Nick kept saying how brave Baby B was and I think Baby B believed him. He thinks he can just walk up to Oyin and catch her.'

'Stuff and nonsense!' Mr Edgar said. 'Oyin will tear them to pieces. Where could they have gone?'

'Round Rock Island,' Philip said.

'What?' thundered Mr Edgar.

'Yes, I'm sure of it. Baby B thinks Oyin is hiding there. He said we could go there and fight her.'

'Oh my hat! He's not going to swim there, surely.'

'No, he said something about a boat.'

Mr Edgar groaned and sat down in a chair. He opened his mouth to speak but then closed it again and shook his head. Philip looked out of the window. The rain was pouring down from the black sky. The wind was blowing so hard that the tops of the trees looked as if they might snap off. Philip could just imagine how rough the sea would be.

'Can you show me where the boat is, Mr Edgar?' Philip asked, pulling the map out of his pocket.

Mr Edgar peered at the map and then pointed to the three houses where the rabbits lived. 'Just here, where the River Busy runs into the sea. The rabbits keep it in a little shed next to this house. It's only a small boat and it hasn't been used for years.'

Philip looked at the map. Baby B and Nick must have started at least fifteen minutes before. He'd never be able to catch them up. But he must do something. He couldn't just leave them alone with Oyin out there. He pointed to the map.

'Look, Mr Edgar – if they're going to try to sail to Round Rock Island, they'll have to go along the coast. If I run very fast, I can probably reach the beach opposite the island about the same time as they do. Perhaps I'll be able to call them and make them come back.'

'Hold on, young 'un, that could be just what Oyin is waiting for. Remember, her last attack will be by Water. And she'll be desperate. She knows what will happen to her if she fails.'

'But if I don't go, she'll attack Baby B and Nick. I must go.'

Mr Edgar took Philip's hand and looked him in the eye. 'You know what?' said the old beaver. 'You're just about one of the bravest young animals it's been my good fortune to meet. Now, get cracking. And just one piece of advice. This will be Oyin's worst attack, but there's a reason she has left it to last. She hates Water. She's made up of Air and Fire. Water is her deadly enemy. In fact, she hates it so much that she won't even want to come out in this rain she's made.'

Philip felt his heart begin to pound. If he waited a moment longer, he would be too afraid to go. He grabbed a torch off the wall.

'Goodbye,' he called to Mr Edgar.

'Good luck, young 'un.'

Philip held the flaming torch up high and started down the stairs.

As he ran along the tunnel, Philip remembered the first time he had used this secret passage. He had been facing danger then, too, but at least no one had known he was coming. This time was different. This time Oyin knew.

And she was out there, just waiting.

CHAPTER TWENTY-ONE

The dark tunnel went on and on. The light of the torch didn't shine very far and the shadows jumped in a very scaring way. Philip was glad when he reached the steps at the end.

The rain hit him in the face as he came out and the wind nearly knocked him over. He put his head down and ran along the path through the forest.

Twigs and small branches fell on him. His feet splashed into puddles and twice he nearly slipped and fell. Already his clothes were soaking wet.

'Still, I mustn't mind the rain,' he thought. 'If Mr Edgar is right, it means that Oyin won't want to come out while it is wet.'

A second later, the rain stopped.

Philip stood still. It was as though Oyin had read his mind. She must know that he had left the safety of Beaver Towers. She had stopped the rain so that she could leave her hiding place and come to look for him.

Huge black clouds were racing across the sky, driven by the wind. Perhaps Oyin was up there, ready to dive down and get him.

Suddenly, he was very scared. He looked behind him along the path. It would be so easy to turn round and go back to the castle. He would be safe there.

No, he must go on.

He felt the wind push him in the back. It wanted him to go on towards the sea. It blew harder and he began to move. The wind howled and pushed. Faster and faster. Soon, he was running and he couldn't stop – Oyin's wind wouldn't let him. Like it or not, he was being blown towards the sea.

He passed the path that led to Mrs Badger's house. He passed the end of the forest. The wind chased him across the open fields. His legs pounded on and on.

There was the Manor. But the wind didn't want him to go that way. It pushed him towards the orchards. Apples and leaves fell on him as he dashed by.

Now he could hear the roar of the sea. He reached the top of a small hill and fell down on to the golden sand.

He lay on the beach. At last he was out of the wind. He sat up and tried to get his breath back. Huge waves were crashing onto the sand. The air was filled with spray. Philip screwed up his eyes and looked out across the angry sea. There was

Round Rock Island. Waves were bursting against it, almost covering it with white foam.

The wind. The waves. It was all part of Oyin's trap. And Oyin's wind had blown him into it like a fly into a spider's web.

What was she going to do? Mr Edgar had said that she was afraid of water. And yet the last attack would be by water. Oh, why wasn't he safe at home?

And where were Baby B and Nick? He couldn't see a boat. Perhaps they had given up the crazy plan to sail to the island. Perhaps they had gone home. He decided to wait for ten minutes then walk to the rabbits' houses to see if they were there.

The wind whistled and roared. The waves broke with a boom. Bits of sand blew through the air and stung his face. He closed his eyes and listened to the noise.

Then, very faintly, he heard it – a tiny, faraway cry for help.

He stood up and looked. He caught a glimpse of something out in the sea but then it was hidden by a big wave. He stood on tiptoe. There it was again. It rose up the side of another wave and he saw it clearly. A small boat. And Baby B and Nick were in it.

'Baby B! Nick!' he called, as he ran down to the edge of the water.

'Flipip! Help!' Baby B shouted back across the roaring sea.

The boat looked so tiny. Each time a wave hit

it, Philip was scared it might turn right over. The two little animals were hanging on to the mast as hard as they could. The sail was flapping wildly in the wind. But, in fact, the wind and waves were helping, because the boat was coming nearer and nearer the shore.

Philip waded out into the sea as far as he could. Waves rose and crashed down on him. He could feel the sea pulling at his legs, trying to knock him over.

The boat came nearer. Another minute and he would be able to grab it and pull it to land.

Nearer and nearer.

A huge wave rolled in. It caught the boat and swished it towards him. He reached out and got hold of the side. At once he started to pull it.

He pulled and pulled.

But the boat didn't seem to move. Surely he must be getting nearer the land? And yet, when he looked, the beach seemed further away.

Yes, it was. The water was getting deeper. He wasn't pulling the boat, the boat was pulling him. His feet could no longer touch the bottom.

The wind had changed. The boat was rushing out to sea and he was going with it.

Suddenly, above the noise of the wind and the sea, he heard another sound. It was the horrible cackling laugh of Oyin. He looked up and saw her. She was flapping her cloak. Each time she flapped it, the wind blew. And each time the wind blew, the boat was carried further and further out to sea.

CHAPTER TWENTY-TWO

The little boat sped away from the shore, rocking like mad. Philip clung on tight as waves burst over him. The water was cold and he could feel his fingers slipping.

'Quick, Flipip. Get in,' Baby B shouted.

Philip took a deep breath and slowly lifted his leg until he got it over the side. The boat tipped and nearly turned over but he slid his body up on to the edge. He felt Baby B pulling. The next minute, he was lying in the bottom of the boat with Baby B and Nick rolling around on top of him.

A giant wave crashed against the boat. Water poured on to them and they tumbled and splashed and bumped into each other. Philip caught hold of the mast and pulled himself up. He grabbed Baby B and Nick and dragged them to the seat at the back of the boat.

They huddled together for warmth and looked

up at Oyin. She pointed a long, bony finger at them and laughed.

'Blow wind,' she suddenly screamed. 'Take them to the island and smash them on the rocks.'

She flapped her cloak and the wind filled the sail. The boat raced towards Round Rock Island. Philip could see the huge waves crashing against the cliffs. In a minute one of those waves would catch the boat. It would hurl them on to the rock and smash them to little pieces.

'What we ... g-g-going t-t-to d-do?' shivered Baby B.

Philip shook his head. What *could* they do?

If only he had a knife to cut the rope that held the sail. If they could get rid of the sail, the wind wouldn't be able to push them nearer the island. He tried pulling the rope but it was too strong.

Then he had an idea.

'Baby B, is it true that beavers can cut down trees with their teeth?' he asked.

'Not very big ones, but only little ones,' said Baby B.

'Do you think you can cut this rope?'

'Easy,' said Baby B.

He bent down and started biting the rope.

The boat was getting nearer the cliffs.

'Hurry up,' shouted Nick, and he grabbed the other side of the rope and started biting, too.

'Ouch, your prickles are prickling my nose,' said Baby B.

'Sorry,' said Nick and he got hold of the end of the rope and pulled instead.

Baby B gave one more bite and the rope broke. The wind caught the canvas and lifted it. The sail tore away from the mast and went flying into the air. The rope went with it. And Nick went with the rope. He had forgotten to let go of the end.

Philip and Baby B could hear the little hedgehog squealing as he was carried away. They watched the sail fly through the air and dive into the sea a long way from the boat.

'Oh, Flipip!' cried Baby B. 'Nick can't swim!'

There was nothing they could do. Now that the sail was gone, the boat had stopped rushing towards the cliffs. But it also meant there was no way they could get to Nick.

'Curse you!' Oyin screamed.

She raised her hands and lightning flashed from her fingertips. Philip grabbed Baby B and threw himself to the front of the boat. The lightning hit the place where they had been standing. The wooden floor cracked and water began to pour in.

If Oyin made another hole like that, the boat would sink in less than a minute. Philip saw her raise her hands again. What could he do? There was only one hope. Perhaps he could trick her.

He stood up and laughed. Oyin looked surprised.

'Go on, send your lightning,' Philip shouted. 'What a stupid witch you are. You can't win with magic. You couldn't get me by Earth, or Air, or Fire. And you won't get me by Water. I've got a magic chain round my neck to stop you. It's more powerful than any magic of yours. You can't hurt me while I've got it.'

There was a long moment while Oyin stared at him. Philip stared back.

Would she believe him? He put one hand near his throat and pretended to touch something there.

'So, silly Oyin. While I've got it round my neck, you can't hurt me. Go back and tell the Prince of Darkness that you have failed again.'

A look of fear crossed Oyin's hideous face. Then she let out a scream and dived.

Philip moved to the edge of the boat. Oyin flew nearer. She had believed him.

Her crooked hands stretched towards his neck.

Philip stood still. He wanted to duck out of the way of those horrible hands. He wanted to hide from that terrible face. But he stood still.

Her fingernails scratched his neck. Philip reached up and grabbed her arms. He held them tight and threw himself backwards.

He saw the terror in Oyin's eyes as she realized what he was doing. A dreadful scream came from her ugly mouth as they both fell into the sea.

Water was her deadly enemy.

Philip felt his hands burning. The sea bubbled and steamed. Oyin's arms jerked and pulled, but Philip held on. It was like fighting an octopus. He felt himself sinking. Deeper and deeper. His lungs were bursting.

Oyin's arms jerked one last time and then stopped moving. Philip let go of her and swam upwards.

He came up by the side of the boat. Baby B helped him climb in. Philip lay down, panting. Slowly, the pain stopped and he opened his eyes.

The sky was blue. The sun was shining.

The wind had stopped and the sea was calm. Oyin's storm was over.

Baby B wiped the water from Philip's face.

'Where did she gone, Flipip?' the little beaver asked in a scared voice.

'I don't know,' said Philip.

They leaned over the side of the boat and looked. The water was very clear and they could see almost to the bottom.

They both gasped as they saw a black shape flapping upwards.

'She's coming again,' said Baby B, and he held on to Philip's hand.

The shape broke the surface. It was Oyin's cloak. It rolled over and there was Oyin. White skull and white bones. Nothing else was left. The water had dissolved her.

She was gone for good.

CHAPTER TWENTY-THREE

The boat was still filling up with water. Philip took off his socks and rolled them into a ball. Then he pushed it as hard as he could into the hole that Oyin's lightning had made.

Baby B was looking very sad and Philip knew that he was thinking about how poor little Nick had been carried away on the sail.

'Come on, Baby B,' he said, 'we must get busy. We've got to get all the water out of the boat or we'll sink.'

Philip gave Baby B one of his shoes and they both started scooping the water out. It took a long time but at last there was only a bit of water left at the bottom.

'Right,' said Philip, 'that's enough. Now we'll have to row back to land.'

Philip took the oars and started rowing. It was slow work because the oars were heavy. Baby B sat at the back of the boat, looking more and more miserable. Soon big tears began to roll down his furry cheeks. Philip felt sad, too. He should have been happy because Oyin was dead and the danger was over but he couldn't help thinking about Nick. And the more he thought about the friendly little hedgehog, the sadder he got.

Philip's eyes filled with tears and he couldn't see properly. What was that floating on the water? It looked like a big sheet. He wiped his eyes and stood up to get a better look. It was the sail. And there was something right in the middle of it. Something that looked like a prickly ball.

It was Nick.

'Nick! Nick!' shouted Philip, jumping up and down so much that the boat nearly tipped over.

The prickly ball started to unroll. A sharp little nose peeped out. Two scared eyes blinked in surprise. Then four little paws started splashing across the wet sail towards the boat. As Nick ran, the soaking sail finally started to sink. The little hedgehog splashed for a moment and then disappeared under the water.

'Quick, Baby B,' Philip yelled.

Baby B didn't need telling twice. He jumped out of the boat and dived under the waves.

There was a long wait. Philip watched. Some bubbles came up and then Baby B appeared, holding Nick in his paws. Philip pulled them both out. Baby B shook his fur and Nick wiggled his spines. Water flew off both of them all over

Philip. But he didn't mind. He started to laugh and Baby B and Nick joined in.

They were still laughing when the boat finally slid on to the golden sand. They jumped out and ran all the way to Beaver Towers.

As they got near the castle, they could see all the animals standing on the walls. They stopped running.

'Let's tell them the good news,' said Philip. 'I'll count to three and then we'll all shout.'

They took a deep breath. Philip counted to three and then they shouted at the top of their voices, 'Oyin is dead!'

You should have heard the cheering and singing and the laughing. It went on until Philip, Baby B and Nick got into the castle. Then it started all over again when Philip told them what had happened. It was still going on when everybody sat down to a huge feast in the evening.

The Great Hall was filled with lights and the tables were piled high with delicious food and drink. After the meal, they played games and then it was time for the dancing.

Philip had never seen a dance like it. Everybody got in a big circle and started clapping. Two by two, the animals rushed into the middle, bumped into each other, fell over and ran back to join the circle. Everybody laughed and cheered and it was so silly that Philip soon found himself laughing too.

When his turn came, Philip ran into the middle

with Baby B. They bumped and fell and laughed and laughed.

The biggest laugh and the loudest cheer came when Mr Edgar and Mrs Badger bumped.

'Oh my hat,' laughed Mr Edgar, as he rolled on the floor, 'I'm getting too long in the tooth for this nonsense. I need a bit of a rest. Fancy some fresh air, young Philip? We can have a chinwag at the same time.'

Mr Edgar led Philip out into the courtyard and up on to the castle walls. They looked out over the forest. The sky was full of stars and the moon was just coming up from behind the mountains.

'Well, young 'un,' Mr Edgar said softly, 'we've got to think about getting you home. And this time we'll make sure your mother and father don't ask awkward questions about where you've been.'

'But they're bound to,' said Philip, 'I've been away even longer than last time.'

'They won't even know you've been out of the house,' Mr Edgar said.

'How?'

'Magic, of course. Been rummaging in my old books and I've found just the spell to do the trick. It'll pop you back to your bedroom a couple of minutes before your mother gets home from seeing – what was the lady's name – the one she went to see the night Oyin paid you a visit?'

'Mrs Jessup?'

'That's the one. So, when your mother opens

the door, she'll find you at home – just as if you've never been away. Topping, eh?'

Philip gulped. 'Can you really do that, Mr Edgar?'

'Of course I can. It'll take me most of tomorrow getting everything ready but I daresay you and that rascally grandson of mine can find some mischief to get up to while you're waiting.'

They both laughed and then Philip suddenly said, 'Oh, Mr Edgar, I will miss you – and Baby B and Mrs Badger and everybody.'

'I know, young 'un – and we'll miss you. It's hard for friends to part. But as long as I can do my magic, there'll always be a way for you to come back. We'll meet again, don't worry.'

Mr Edgar patted Philip on the arm. 'Let's just enjoy tonight. Come along, it's time we went back inside.'

The dancing had finished and all the animals were sitting round the fire telling stories and jokes. And the story that they all wanted to hear again was about how Philip and Baby B and Nick had fought the dreaded witch, Oyin.

Philip told it. Nick told it. Then it was Baby B's turn. And the little beaver decided to tell it and act it at the same time. He ran around the room, jumping on chairs and acting all the parts. But when he finished, Baby B became all serious.

'Grandpa,' he said.

'What is it, little scamp?' said Mr Edgar as Baby B climbed on to his lap.

'If Flipip was naughty, you won't tell him off, will you?'

'Why, what's he done?' said Mr Edgar, puzzled.

'He told a big fibber. He said to Oyin he's got a magic thing on his neck but he didn't really have one.'

Mr Edgar chuckled and stroked the fur on the top of Baby B's head. 'Well, I suppose it was a bit of a fib,' he said gently, 'but I think we can forgive him, don't you?'

Baby B thought deeply for a minute and then said, 'Yes, I think we can because he only did it for a very good reason and usuarally he doesn't tell fibs at all.'

Baby B nodded to himself and thought for a bit. 'Grandpa,' he said at last, 'I think Flipip is the bestest human beak in the whole world, don't you?'

'Yes,' said Mr Edgar. 'I think we all do.'

All the animals looked at Philip and he was so embarrassed that he didn't know what to say.

Someone started humming a song. Everybody joined in and soon the hall was filled with gentle music. Baby B came over and snuggled up on Philip's lap.

The dangerous adventure was over.

The fire glowed in the fireplace and the soft song went on and on. Each animal was making his own sound. There were no words, but Philip knew what the song was about.

It was about trees and winds and sun and sea. And most of all it was about friends and love.